PENDRAGON

AND THE

CLASH OF KINGDOMS

C.J. BROWN

PENDRAGON LEGEND
BOOK FOUR:

PENDRAGON AND THE CLASH OF KINGDOMS

JOIN C.J. BROWN'S NEWSLETTER AT CJ-BROWN.COM

CONTENTS

For my fans--you make storytelling a joy.

1

THE DAWN OF WAR

A GREAT FOG HUNG OVER PITTENTRAIL as a light rain turned the dirt roads to mud. Sand washed away from the cobblestone paths as fires warmed the guards who manned the watchtowers.

King Fergus sat furious in his court, a fire crackling in the hearth and the sconces.

Suddenly, the great wooden doors opened, and the captain of the guard ran in, tired from the run from the wall to the palace.

"Your Grace," he said, dropping to his knee, "the trespasser escaped. But we hit him with an arrow."

"What?" Fergus bellowed. "What happened to my daughter?"

1

The captain did not look at the Highlander king.

"She is gone, Your Grace, captured by the trespasser."

King Fergus remained silent. His anger boiled as his eyes showed the fire of his soul. He stared at the captain.

"We will find them," he swore at last.

"Arthur was the trespasser, Your Grace," the captain said. "It was Lord Gallagher who hit him."

Arthur?" Fergus said. "Arthur was the trespasser?"

"Yes, Your Grace."

"How did your men not know he was here?"

"I'm sorry, Your Grace, they just couldn't see him."

"Arrest them," Fergus said. "Then resign your post."

The captain looked at his king.

Fergus was boiling with rage. Only great will kept him from drawing his sword and cutting the captain down where he knelt.

"Yes, Your Grace," the man said, and withdrew.

"Gallagher," Fergus said, "my spies tell me Arthur's band left Inver Ridge for Demetia. You will lead an army there. Burn his body and bring me his head."

Gallagher smirked.

"Yes, Your Grace."

2

PYRES AND GOODBYES

I ARTHUR REMAINED STILL AS THE cart horse walked on, Merlin with his horse just a few yards away, watching the scene.

Arthur knew what had happened.

Blood still poured from his wound that hurt every time the horse moved and when he breathed.

The mild rain diluted the blood as it dripped to the grass.

Arthur's eyes showed the loss, the pain he was feeling. It was nothing like he had ever felt before. No battle wound, no insult, had ever hurt Arthur as much as the loss of the only woman he had ever loved.

As the horse approached Merlin, the wizard retrieved another cloak that glowed crimson from his robe.

"Here," he said. "It will not be long before they find us."

Covering Arthur and Olivie with the cloak, they disappeared as the horse continued to walk.

"We make for Demetia," Merlin said.

The horse suddenly began galloping towards the mountain pass that led to the open plains.

Merlin followed.

By sunset, the two horses were at the enchanted forest.

Verovingian appeared to greet them, along with Magi Ro Hul.

By the look on Merlin's face, things had gone terribly wrong.

"Where are Arthur and Olivie?" Magi asked.

Merlin turned and removed the cloak.

"No," Magi Ro Hul said, looking at Arthur and Olivie, seeing the arrow that had hit them.

Merlin turned to Arthur, his cloak still crimson.

"Arthur, I have to remove the arrow," he said.

Arthur did not respond. His eyes were closed.

Merlin, still astride his horse, reached over, held Arthur with one hand, and pulled the arrow with the other.

The former Pendragon winced as the blade cut through his flesh again but held Olivie to keep her from falling.

His eyes open, he looked first at Magi Ro Hul, who was fuming with rage and grief.

4

Arthur got down from the horse, holding Olivie in his arms. Placing her on the grass, he knelt amidst the trees that shielded them from the storm.

He collapsed.

He awoke and saw the ceiling of the wooden structure. A hearth burned brightly near the foot of his bed. Sconces illuminated the room, and two windows allowed Arthur to look out at the night. Rain and mist blurred the sight of the city outside.

At first, having forgotten what had happened, the memories of the day then rushed back to him.

Tears welling in his eyes, he tried to keep his composure. But he could not, not against a pain beyond any by which he had ever been tested.

He wept.

But a knock on the wooden doors to his right stopped him.

He wiped the tears away.

"Enter," he said.

Merlin stepped in.

"Friend," he began, "it is time. My father, your mother, the entire court, and the citizens have gathered. The armor of a Demetian general has been prepared for you.

Arthur nodded, understanding.

"I'll be out in a moment."

Merlin nodded and left.

Arthur rose from his bed, surprised to find his wound already healed. How long had it been?

Walking to the stand where his Demetian armor was, he eyed the polished iron.

Donning the chainmail, the greaves, and the sabatons, he fitted the cuirass and then picked up the great halfhelm. Inspired by the Spartans, it was symbolic of the Demetians' ability to fight.

He wore the helmet, and then buckled on the greatsword, swearing to use the blade to fell Bishkar, and all who had destroyed his family.

Emerging from his room, he found the wooden corridor empty and walked to the stairwell at the other end. He hurried down the steps, lit by sconces.

He emerged into a common area, where two tattooed guards manned the entrance.

They cleared the way of their spears to let Arthur pass, then turned to follow him.

Outside, rain was pouring. Thunder roared overhead as lightning clapped.

A great torrent bathed the land, but the city of Demetia was shielded from the worst of it by the enchanted forest.

A solemn choir song was sounding from the distance, where a ring of sconces burned. More than a thousand people were standing there, their heads bowed.

Arthur moved with rage and grief, followed by the two royal guards. No chatter was maintained by the crowd.

As Arthur approached the site, he saw King Megolin standing by his seat, atop a dais. Igraine was there too, as was Merlin, and Magi Ro Hul.

As he walked toward them, Merlin turned to see him.

Arthur reached the crowd, who began moving to clear a path to the dais.

He walked toward the platform and stepped up.

He stopped when he saw Olivie, surrounded by flowers. Her wound could not be seen, but she was pale, absent.

Merlin said nothing as Igraine watched the scene with sorrow.

Megolin felt Arthur's pain as well. His own beloved had left him decades ago, felled by a sickness not even his father, the greatest of Demetia's warlocks, could cure. It was a sickness of the mind, one that Igraine had been there to see.

For Igraine, the way Arthur felt about the loss of Olivie was the way she had felt when she left Uther. He was just as lost.

Arthur stared at the only woman he had ever loved as he walked to stand beside Magi Ro Hul.

Silent, he stared at the closed eyes of Olivie, and a tear rolled down his cheek.

The pain of his broken family, of his lost father, of the tragedy Bishkar had brought upon his family, all rushed to his attention.

The choir completed their solemn verses and the high priest stepped forward from a dais adjacent to the royal platform.

"Gods, warlocks of old, ancestors of King Megolin of

Demetia, we call upon you to bless the soul of this fallen princess. A foreigner, she is yet a child of Gaea. Thus, she passes to the afterlife with your blessing. But for her honor, we call Magi Ro Hul, a friend, to bid farewell according to the customs of the Highlanders."

The priest, his robe an ocean blue, his long hair a simple gray, motioned to Magi Ro Hul.

The Highlander warrior, the first northern general to visit Demetia in fifty years, descended the dais, and stood a foot from Olivie.

Wiping the tear that rolled from his eye, he raised his hands, and looked up at the rustling canopy, the sound of the rain lessening as thunder continued to roar.

"All gods of nature," he said, "a life is lost. Dear to many, her soul now joins the souls of all who have passed. She was felled not by sickness nor by grief, but by the arrow of one of her own people."

Magi Ro Hul lowered his arms.

"I swear vengeance," he said.

Magi Ro Hul turned to return to his place.

"Now, Arthur, the loved one of Olivie," the priest said.

Arthur turned to Magi Ro Hul as he stood beside him, his face cold.

With his Demetian cape trailing behind, Arthur walked toward Olivie.

His armor clinked as he walked, the hilt of his longsword reflecting the fires that crackled around Olivie.

Passing between two of the torches, he stood a foot from her.

A long silence reigned, broken only by the falling rain and the song of crickets.

"Please forgive me, my love," he finally said. "May the gods have mercy on my soul, for I will not rest till Bishkar, till the man who killed you, till all those who have destroyed my family have paid."

He removed his gauntlet and held her hand, both of her arms folded and resting, holding a lily.

Unable to hold back his tears, he wept silently.

King Megolin remained silent.

Merlin observed. He had never seen anyone grieve like this. Even when his own mother died, his father had not been like this. His father just continued being king. Peace was still being negotiated with the Highlanders at the time.

The neutral land between Demetia and Caledonia was being established. Megolin had had no time to weep. Merlin had grieved in his own way, focusing on practicing his spells, his magic.

But never had he seen a man grieve like Arthur was grieving now.

Arthur turned and returned to the dais.

Igraine looked at him, tears rolling from her eyes. She knew it was the greatest pain her son had ever endured.

"Be strong," she said to him.

He nodded but did not otherwise respond.

Igraine felt there was almost nothing she could do now.

Arthur needed time, and all the support he could have. Against a derailed father, a reviled half-brother, without a name, and lost, Arthur would not be the same person he was when they sailed for Britannia, just a moon ago.

"Light the pyre," the priest said.

A pair of royal guards picked up two torches, walked to the pyre, and held the flame to the wooden twigs. It took a moment for the fire to reach the dry layer. Then the pyre began to burn, and smoke rose up.

Arthur's tears reflected the fire as he felt his rage rising, and his hand gripped the hilt of his longsword.

Less than an hour later, while the fire continued to burn, Arthur hurried to King Megolin's great hall.

Merlin and Megolin followed, along with Igraine. Magi Ro Hul was with them too.

Standing before the throne of King Megolin, the lord of Demetia seated himself in his place. Merlin stood beside him, flanked by Igraine, and Arthur before them, with Magi Ro Hul to his side.

The dry hall, warmed by the sconces and great hearth, was silent but for the crackling of the fire.

Arthur remained silent for a moment. All of them did.

Then he removed his halfhelm. "Your Grace," he said, kneeling before the king, "my father, Uther Pendragon, has allied with the Hun general, Bulanid Mehmet. He has been renamed Gallagher Pendragon. King Fergus betrothed Olivie to him. Uther sees me as his enemy. He

10

sees my mother as his enemy. Anyone who opposes him is his enemy.

"There is a good chance Attila still plans to invade Britannia. Olivie told me how Bulanid defeated a Hun army at Dornoch, slaying their leader, Lispania. Those ten thousand, most of whom are now his prisoners, his warriors, are expendables. They are just the men the Huns use to weaken their enemy before attacking with the main force.

"That is the army Attila will send to attack the isle. Uther will most likely use Gallagher to attack me and those friendly to me. War is brewing, and the Hun invasion cannot be stopped if we are fighting the Highlanders."

Arthur returned to silence as the rest of them contemplated what he was saying.

"We have to warn King Fergus, then," Megolin said.

"I'm afraid he will not listen," Arthur responded. "He will blame me for Olivie's death. He has grown close to Gallagher, respectful of that snake's staged victory. He has grown close to Uther, as Gallagher is his heir. He will stand against us."

"We cannot afford a war with the Highlanders," Merlin added.

"I assure you, our armies and our people wish it not," Magi said.

"You must return your father to his senses," Igraine said. "Your father is the only one who can stop the war between our people and the Highlanders from resuming. If he advises Fergus against it, he may listen. But it will be a difficult task. Your father has strayed far from the path of wisdom and honor. He now seeks only revenge. Motivated by pain, he will not stop till what he perceives has caused that pain is gone. You must return your father to himself."

Arthur nodded, realizing the difficulty of the task at hand. "Yes, Mother."

"I will head back to Pittentrail," Magi Ro Hul said. "My men are loyal to me. I will make sure they do not go to war against Demetia or you. We will focus our efforts on the Huns. But I do not control our fleet. Admiral Muireach is loyal to Fergus."

"Do your best," Arthur said.

"Aye. I shall leave at once."

The Highlander general bowed before the royals and left by the great doors.

"King Megolin," Arthur said, after a moment. "If I may, I request a thousand of your best soldiers, all horse. We will head to Pittentrail. We will avoid fighting as much as we can. The mission is for me to speak with my father and bring him back."

Megolin pondered the request. It was a great risk. War was not something Demetia could afford.

"Fine," he finally said.

"Call General Clyde to the great hall!" He shouted to the guards at the door.

"Yes, Your Grace," one of them said, and left.

In a moment, the general marched into the hall, his

sabatons striking the wooden floor as his cloak trailed behind him, his helmet held between his arm and his side.

"You sent for me, Your Grace?"

"Transfer a thousand of your best cavalrymen to Arthur," the king said. "Prepare them to leave in an hour."

"Yes, Your Grace," Clyde said, bowing his head as a drop of water fell from his long, silver beard.

The general left and the doors closed.

"I take my leave," Arthur declared, to the royal Megolin family.

"I shall follow," Merlin said. "A thousand cloaks will be supplied to shield our force."

"Yes," Megolin agreed.

"Be careful, Arthur," Igraine said. "The lives of all those here, and all who inhabit this isle are now uncertain. What happens henceforth is in your control."

"Yes, Mother," Arthur said, the weight of the responsibility he carried growing painful on his shoulders.

Arthur bowed to Megolin.

Then he rose and walked to the doors as Merlin followed, his cloak glowing red.

Outside, the rain had stopped. The neighing of horses could be heard as Clyde bellowed the command to assemble in the courtyard.

The smoke of Olivie's pyre could be seen in the distance, but Arthur could not look.

Still, he felt his anger rise, and he walked toward the courtyard, following Merlin.

His sabatons and cloak picking up mud as he left the palatial area, he could see cavalry trotting toward the courtyard, pennons, and the flag of Megolin streaming in the wind that chilled the city.

The clouds were clearing, allowing moon and starlight to shine on the cobblestone and dirt roads.

As they approached the courtyard, Merlin stopped and turned to him.

"I must depart. A thousand cloaks for the horsemen and ourselves will be supplied momentarily."

Arthur nodded, and Merlin left.

As Arthur arrived at the courtyard encircled by wooden and stone buildings, more cavalry piled in from the western and northern barracks.

"Handpicked, my lord," Clyde said, standing beside a guard post as he watched the cavalry assemble.

"Good," Arthur said.

"My sympathies for your loss," he added.

Arthur turned to him.

"I lost my wife during the last war with the Highlanders, fifty years ago. They had launched a raid. This very courtyard was burning.

"I have learned to make peace with my loss, and not to look upon the Highlanders with hate. I assure you, my lord, it is a far better path than anger."

"I appreciate your words," Arthur said, turning back to the cavalry as the last riders formed the battalion.

Clyde motioned for Arthur to address the men.

"Men!" Arthur shouted. "Warriors of Demetia! King Megolin has entrusted me with your lives. You are the best horsemen this kingdom has. But war or battle is not our objective. We are to reach Pittentrail. Cloaks supplied by Merlin will be used to hide our approach. You will surround the city. Do not attack even if they arrest me. Only do so if I launch a burning arrow, or if Bulanid attacks with his Huns. You will recognize their foul faces from a mile away. Uther, my father, is the man I seek to return to reason. Do not attack him for any reason. Understood?"

"Yes, my lord," they all shouted back.

Merlin appeared, almost out of nowhere.

"Wear these," Merlin said, just loud enough for everyone to hear.

One by one, the horsemen and their horses disappeared as they wrapped themselves in Merlin's special cloaks, meant for their horses as well. Passed around by servants, all that was soon seen was an empty courtyard.

"Dawn will be here in three hours," Merlin told Arthur.

The Roman nodded.

"Here is your horse," Verovingian said, walking up to them with Boadicea and Merlin's horse. "And the horn of Demetia. Sound it thrice when you return should there be danger."

"Thank you, friend," Arthur said, and walked over.

"May Gaea watch over you," Verovingian said.

Arthur nodded before taking the horn, placing his armored feet in the stirrups, and vaulting up onto his horse.

Merlin passed him a cloak just as King Megolin and Igraine appeared at the end of one of the streets leading to the courtyard.

They stepped up to the dais.

"May Gaea watch over you," Megolin said.

"Goodbye, Your Grace. Goodbye, Mother."

Merlin ascended his destrier and wrapped the cloak around himself.

He disappeared.

Arthur, seeing through his halfhelm, wrapped the glowing cloak around his torso and horse.

He turned Boadicea around. Connected by the cloaks, he could see the horsemen again, and they cleared a path as he rode to the front.

Merlin followed behind, and within minutes they were leading the battalion out of the forest.

They emerged outside and beheld the rolling plains of Demetia as the moon set in the west.

Invisible to all others, the thousand horsemen followed as Arthur broke into a gallop, headed for Pittentrail.

3

THE OTHER SIDE OF TREASON

MAGI RO HUL STORMED THROUGH the doors of King Fergus' court.

"Your Grace," he said, dropping to his knee.

"Magi Ro Hul, where have you been?" The king bellowed.

"I travel from Demetia. Olivie is no longer with us."

Fergus' face turned pale as the members of his court looked at the general.

"The arrow that hit Arthur hit her as well," Magi said, boiling himself.

"It was Gallagher who fired that arrow."

Magi looked at Fergus. "What?" he said.

"I'm sorry, Your Grace, that was not my intention," Gallagher said.

Magi Ro Hul turned and saw him standing at the entrance. Just the look of the barbarian was enough to turn the great general cold. He eyed him cruelly.

"I truly did not mean for that," Gallagher said, ignoring Magi Ro Hul.

Fergus stared at the heir to the Empire.

"Is your army ready to depart?" King Fergus asked.

"Yes, sire," Gallagher said, much to Magi Ro Hul's worry. "They will depart for Demetia within the hour."

"Magi Ro Hul," Fergus said, "call the army to arms. March for Demetia. This time, there will be no negotiations."

Magi Ro Hul looked at him. The King Fergus he knew the day Arthur arrived had long since passed. He stared only at a madman. "Yes, Your Grace," he said, tasting bile at the back of his throat.

He turned to leave the court, followed by Gallagher.

Passing the guards as he made his way to the stairwell, he considered what he was about to do. His king had ordered him to deploy the army. Gallagher was preparing to set out for Demetia, and he was to lead ten thousand men alongside him. Fergus knew Demetia had allied with Arthur, and the Highlander king was not hesitant to restart the war that had lasted generations and took decades to end.

Passing the prime minister's and the other council members' official chambers, he reached the front doors, guarded by two dressed in gold.

He hurried to sound the gongs and ring the bells.

Captains and lieutenants assembled in the commanders' hall.

"His Grace has ordered us to march for Demetia," he said, solemnly.

None of the officers liked what they were hearing. He was counting on it.

"Lord Gallagher and his army will be heading there as well. Demetia's forces number only five thousand. They will not be able to hold out against twenty thousand Highlanders and Huns."

Chatter suddenly erupted as the officers realized they would be marching with Huns, the reviled rejects of the known world.

"Silence!" Magi Ro Hul boomed, and so it fell on the hall.

With only the sound of the fire crackling in the hearths, the Highlander general eyed his men.

"We will march for Demetia," he said. "And we will defend them. We will attack when the time is right."

The men stayed silent.

What their general was contemplating was treason, punishable by death. The alternative was a war that would break the peace that had till now been secure.

"Aye, my lord," Captain Holdsbar stood up. "We will

follow you, if it is for the good of our people, and for all people."

"Aye," another said.

"Aye," the rest of the officers one by one agreed.

Magi Ro Hul eyed the wisdom and the loyalty of his men with relief. But he knew what they were promising. Should they fail, should King Fergus fail to see reason, things far worse than death would be served to them, for these men valued honor and peace more than they did their lives.

"However, no matter what," Magi Ro Hul said, "do not harm Lord Uther."

Within the hour, horns were roaring from the watchtowers as officers shouted orders. Soldiers on foot, marching with their spears and swords, filed out of the city as cavalry trotted out. Banners and pennons streamed in the wind as the Highlander army amassed outside the gates.

Magi Ro Hul watched from atop his cart horse as two thousand horse and eight thousand foot marched out in three columns.

The sun was approaching its zenith. A cool breeze rustled the trees and the grass.

The army would be at Demetia by the witching hour.

Magi Ro Hul turned and saw with anger that Gallagher, clad in the armor of Arthur, his cape falling from his horse, led nine thousand Hun prisoners, all dressed in Highlander attire, out of the city, with Uther beside him.

Magi Ro Hul straightened. He knew Arthur was setting out to meet with his father.

The Roman eagle streamed in the wind as Hun standard-bearers marched among the two legions Gallagher had divided them into.

Magi Ro Hul turned back to his men.

The cavalry was at the front, all holding their spears and waiting for their general's command.

Captains and lieutenants sat astride their horses, apart from the cavalry phalanxes, while infantry commanders stood aside from their men. All of them knew their true plan. None of them had disagreed.

"Men!" Magi Ro Hul shouted as he rode before the cavalry. "Soldiers of Caledonia! Highlanders! Today, we attack the accursed Southrons who dare challenge our rule! They harbor a greater enemy, the lost son of the heir to the Roman Empire! Today, we seize him, and today, we fight for the glory of Pittentrail, for the honor of our fathers, and for all those who died in our wars with them!"

"Yah!" The Highlanders bellowed. Even the guards atop the walls cheered. Soldiers beat their shields as the cavalrymen raised their spears.

Magi Ro Hul turned to Gallagher.

From afar, the Hun general watched the scene with anger.

"How dare he make a claim to the glory that should be mine?" He bellowed, thinking of his hatred for Arthur.

"They will fail," Uther said. "The glory will be ours. Justice will be served."

"Quite true," Gallagher responded as trebuchet crews emerged with their catapults.

There was a total of a dozen, six amongst the Hun army, and six amongst the Highlander force, with wagons carrying buckets of tar following, the horses neighing as they pulled their burdens forward.

Magi Ro Hul looked back at his men.

He drew his greatsword, the light of the sun reflecting in the fullers of his blade and the gems that formed the eyes of the pommel, carved in the likeness of a wolf.

He turned his horse towards the mountain pass only Highlanders knew how to traverse. Then he swung his sword toward the mountainside and broke into a gallop.

The army cheered as the ranks of cavalry followed, their hooves shaking the ground while the infantry ran behind. The horses dragging the trebuchets and wagons of tar raced forward, trained for stamina, distance, and speed despite their burden.

***

Gallagher watched as the Highlander army raced toward the mountain pass, angry that Magi Ro Hul had set out before him.

"Charge!" he shouted.

Uther galloped towards the pass while the Hun expendables ran after the two riders, leaving the trebuchets rolling slowly behind.

Dropping their banners as they ran, they thundered towards the pass as if they were attacking an enemy.

In minutes, the Highlander column had thinned to lines of ten and were steadily but hastily making their way out of the valley.

***

Magi Ro Hul charged for the top of the road, his horse expertly maneuvering through the dirt, roots, and rocks. Loose dirt and smooth granite made the ascent dangerous, presenting opportunities to slip.

But the Highlander warhorses and the men on foot knew their way and were thundering across the rolling plains by noon. The catapults arrived later, filing out of the pass one by one.

Gallagher's army was nowhere to be seen.

C.J. BROWN

4

THE RISE OF THE HUNS

LATE AFTERNOON WAS KIND TO the Huns and the Franks of occupied Paris. A cool breeze disturbed the shops along the Sequena River, where Hun soldiers and Franks themselves were buying food, clothing, and jewelry from the shop-owners. The Huns used the gold they'd looted from the city, willing to be more humane than they'd ever been.

Merchants from Italy were buying and selling at the busy river that had caused the creation of this great city.

The city was alive with chatter, but none of the Franks were smiling.

Attila watched the activity of the day with impatience, waiting for news.

Then the great doors to his chambers opened, and hurried footsteps were heard.

Attila turned and darted back from the balcony.

The lone Hun panted to regain his breath. "I bring news from the isle, Your Grace," he said.

By the tone of his voice and the look of his face, Attila knew something had gone wrong. "Speak," he said.

"General Lispania's forces were defeated at Dornoch. Nine thousand were taken prisoner. We were ambushed while they were still debarking. The enemy commander told me I was to send a message."

"What message?" Attila asked, raging with anger.

"'I am Arthur.'"

Attila stared at the messenger, his fiery eyes looking directly at the man's soul.

"And what of Bishkar?" He asked, quietly.

"I know nothing, Your Grace."

"Sound the drums," Attila said. "Send for Gerlach."

In moments, the drums were beating, calling for the assembly of the twenty-thousand Hun warriors and the twenty-thousand Frank prisoners they had made expendables. Gerlach appeared at the door. The guards recoiled at his movement, moving aside to let the Hun commander walk.

His right eye was scarred and white. Battle scars lined his face. A section of his scalp where fire had burned him appeared gnarled and deformed. His hair was a thin layer, hanging from his head to his ears.

Attila could smell his breath from two feet away.

His flared nose huffed as he walked over, the Hun insignia tattooed on his face. Tattered fur cloaks clothed him. They all reeked of mead and filth.

"Your Grace," he said, bowing before the shorter Hun, his guttural voice echoing.

"Gerlach, you are now general of my armies. Lispania has failed. Arthur, the same Roman filth who killed your father, killed him. You are to lead the invasion. Call the ships from Le Havre. Lead the Huns to the shores of Britannia. Find Arthur. Capture him and kill all who try to stop you."

Gerlach smirked. "Yes, Your Grace."

The seven-foot giant turned and left, while Attila returned to the balcony to see thousands of Hun warriors marching through the streets of Paris.

The drums continued to beat as captains loaded their men onto the line of triremes and galleys, a few more having been built along the Sequena by the Frank slaves. The expendables were lashed with ropes as they walked across the gangplanks.

Slaves, chained to their oars, sat ready to row out to the channel.

As a crow left Paris, bound for Le Havre with a message, nine hundred men each crammed aboard the triremes and commandeered Frank ships.

Captains bellowed orders as the Huns prepared to leave.

Gerlach was watching the soldiers form their ranks with joy. He had been fighting for Attila since he was a tween. His father had been a general, and he was commander of the expendables. He knew not who Lispania was, only that he was just another one of the thousands he once commanded. Now, he led forty thousand Huns. By the time they landed on the coast of Britannia, the fleet from Le Havre would've landed as well.

Then, he would lead fifty thousand Hun warriors and expendables. All the tribes, all the kingdoms, all the people of Britannia would bow to the mighty Huns.

Gerlach relished the prospect. A skilled warrior, his chipped gladius, captured from a Roman general he had slain, had long been ready for battle. The long repose they had had at Paris had turned the thirty-year-old impatient for war.

5

LEGION OF ROME

TIBERIUS WATCHED THE CITY OF Paris from his warhorse, the plume of his helmet rustling in the wind.

His crimson cape flowed from his back, the crest of his family embossed on his cuirass. Bucephalus, as he had named his horse, neighed as he watched the Hun army preparing for departure.

Suddenly, a Hun rider appeared a hundred yards away, thundering toward the Roman legion.

Tiberius watched as the five thousand legionaries and cavalry stood to attention behind him, the banners of Rome's armies streaming in the wind.

The lone rider stopped just a few feet away.

"His Grace, King Attila has been aware of your presence since you began tracking us," the Hun said.

Tiberius grew angry. It was an insult to his ability.

"He calls you to join his forces that are now departing for Britannia. He calls you to join the attack. But Arthur and Uther are his. He promises Rome will regain the land it once held across the Narrow Sea."

Tiberius glared at the rider.

"I will consult the emperor," he said.

"Very well. You have three days."

The Hun messenger turned and rode off, back to Paris.

Tiberius turned angrily to a messenger who was already walking toward him.

"Send word to Emperor Lucius. Ask him for approval."

"Yes, my lord," the Roman said.

Vaulting onto his Berber, he galloped past the legion, and then turned straight for Rome.

6

THE RECKONING

THEY HAD NOT STOPPED BUT to water their horses.

Now, with the sun past its zenith, the unseen battalion still charged north.

They were almost at Inver Ridge.

Arthur, still raging with grief and anger, had gone ahead of the Demetian cavalry. Eagles soared above them.

Arthur looked up and thought of Alexander who saw the eagle at the Battle of Gaugamela, perceiving that Zeus was on his side.

As the thousand and two horses raced through the grass and the trees, passing towns and hamlets, Arthur noticed the kingdom he had not seen the few times he had traveled from Inver Ridge to Demetia, and from Pittentrail to Megolin's kingdom.

It was a humble city. Stone watchtowers surrounded it as guards walked the parapets. He could not see beyond that.

It was one of the sixteen tribes the emissary Emperor Constantine III sent to survey Britannia and its people had cataloged. Arthur paid no more attention to it when he heard Merlin's voice in his head.

"Magi Ro Hul approaches," he said, "but not far ahead of foes."

Arthur looked out at the horizon.

There was nothing.

Then a lone rider appeared, followed by lines of charging horses numbering five hundred. Banners and pennons were flying in the wind.

Arthur recognized they were Highlanders, and felt relief that Magi Ro Hul had succeeded, but worry that he was leading an army ready for war.

Then he saw a second line of cavalry appear.

They flew the Roman and Hun banner, the sight of which sickened Arthur to his core, to see the colors of his people flying beside those of the vilest known to man.

Two riders led the charge, both clad in Roman attire.

He recognized one of them as his own.

He pulled his reins, and Boadicea neighed as she reared.

Halting as Merlin and the thousand Demetian riders

raced toward him, he watched as the Hun and Highlander armies approached, just a league away.

Merlin stopped beside Arthur, and the Demetian warriors stopped a few yards behind, their horses neighing.

"Magi Ro Hul did not betray us," Arthur said. "Either he has a plan, or that isn't him."

"That is Magi Ro Hul," Merlin said. "He has a plan. He will attack Bulanid and Uther on the way to Demetia."

Arthur paled as he watched the two armies charge.

"Father," he muttered.

"He is in pain," Merlin responded. "All he needs is his family and affirmation that his sins are in his past, that he is a new person. Once, he was loyal to his greed. Now, he truly is loyal to the throne and to honor."

Arthur did not respond.

The approaching armies were now half a league away.

"We follow them. Either we initiate the attack against the Huns, or Magi Ro Hul will."

Merlin nodded and commanded the men silently.

At once, they began moving aside and Arthur turned to follow as they watched the approaching forces draw near.

Clearing the way for the Highlanders and the Huns to pass, they watched as thousands of horses thundered past, followed by infantry who ran.

The Highlander trebuchets were being pulled by powerful horses. The Hun army was more disorganized, with their men running out of formation, their catapults moving slowly.

A gap of a thousand yards separated the infantry from the cavalry.

All stood in silence as the armies roared past.

Then Arthur broke into a gallop and raced to follow, leading Demetians.

No one from the other armies could hear them over the sound of their own horses thundering and men shouting.

Within an hour, the two forces were slowing, and Arthur kept pace.

Horses neighed and snickered as the Huns stopped along one bank of a stream, and the Highlanders along the other.

Arthur stopped, signaling the Demetians to halt.

The Hun cavalry warriors got off their horses to wash their faces with the water of the river while their horses drank.

They ate, and the Highlanders did the same, but they were not as relaxed as the Huns. They were watching, and Magi Ro Hul was still astride his cart horse.

"They are going to attack now," Arthur said to Merlin. "Be ready."

They watched from the Hun bank as the Highlanders prepared to spring the trap.

Arthur led the invisible battalion closer to the site.

Then a horn blared, and the Highlanders jumped up,

drawing their swords. They rushed across the river as archers released a shower of arrows.

Arthur threw off his cloak and drew his greatsword, shouting.

He charged, and those who followed him shrugged off their cloaks, revealing a thousand warriors who rushed to attack the Huns, spears at the ready.

The shower of arrows fell on the Huns as they looked in panic at the Highlander army attacking, and the other cavalry group that had appeared out of nowhere.

Horses ran across the stream as Huns fell, their blood reddening the water. They weren't able to draw their weapons before they were cut down by axes and swords.

Arthur slashed a Hun expendable as he thundered past him. Merlin watched the battle unfold as the Demetian cavalry attacked, mowing down rank upon rank of barbarians.

Arthur was turning all around, cutting down infantry and warriors who had got on horseback again.

His blood-stained armor gleamed in the afternoon sun as he caught sight of Bishkar slashing at the Demetian cavalry attacking him.

Uther was not far away, fighting on foot against Highlander warriors who backed away, knowing they were not supposed to harm him.

Arthur broke into a gallop and headed straight for Uther.

His father watched the horse approach, ready to cut down the rider as he neared.

Arthur sheathed his sword and reached to grab Uther by the shoulder.

Pulled onto his son's horse, the rightful emperor did not know how to respond, and passed out from the force of the capture.

Around Arthur, arrows crisscrossed the sky and air. Shouts sounded as the ring of iron blocked out all other noise.

Highlander cavalry targeted the Hun infantry while soldiers on foot attacked the catapult crews. Two of the trebuchets broke down, and the Huns were beginning to organize. With shouts, Bishkar was reforming his men.

Arthur stopped by the bank of the stream. An arrow suddenly raced past his face, and he turned to see a Hun archer preparing to loose another arrow.

He turned and raced toward him, drawing his sword. Before the archer could react, Arthur slashed the man's armor, causing him to fall from his horse.

Within moments, the battle had escalated. The Huns were no longer defending against an ambush. They were fighting back.

The Highlander warriors fell back from the stream, as Bishkar led a charge against them. Arrows blocked out the sun as they raced toward the Caledonian men.

Arthur could not see Magi Ro Hul.

He turned and saw Merlin watching the battle, his cloak crimson, and his face grim.

Then Arthur watched as the Highlander and Demetian forces were being pushed back.

A horn sounded, and the Highlander cavalry began retreating, charging for Demetia.

Merlin read Arthur's mind and ordered the men to retreat.

In moments, they were racing back to Demetia, Uther slumped unconscious behind Arthur, tied to Boadicea, as Bishkar pursued them, boiling with rage.

***

The three armies thundered across the plains of Britannia.

Archers continued to loose their arrows at the Caledonian and Highlander men as the horses charged.

Arthur galloped at the front line, with Merlin to his side. The beasts pulling the Highlander catapults were still keeping up, and the Hun army was just yards behind. Arrows raced back and forth. Horses and men fell amidst the stampede as the twenty thousand soldiers ran.

The Huns did not relent.

For hours, they charged.

An hour before sunset, Arthur saw the wood-line of the enchanted forest.

He picked up his horn and blew three times.

Rumbles echoed through the forest, disturbing the

leaves. Verovingian looked up at the sound, and then heard the horses.

From behind, horns and trumpets began to blare.

General Clyde stood before an assembling phalanx of cavalry as infantry and horses amassed across the city.

Archers ascended the trees and waited for the enemy to appear. Men prepared catapults as lookouts eyed the charging armies. Shouts rang out from the courtyard as the men readied for battle.

King Megolin hurriedly donned his armor. Chain mail, cuirass, and greaves were thrown on, and he turned to pick up his normar, one of the common helmets modified for royals. The crest of his family embossed on the forehead of his helmet, he put it on and buckled on his longsword, passed down from generations.

His servants backed away, and he turned to leave.

With the men of the royal guard marching behind him, one of them carrying the banner of the House of Megolin, a servant brought him his horse, a mighty destrier of the North. Its hooves struck the cobblestone road as it walked toward him. He held the reins and vaulted up.

His cloak falling over the horse, he placed his feet in the stirrups and turned to gallop toward the courtyard, more cavalry and infantry following him.

Shouts sounded across the city as the city guard evacuated people from the northern sector. Wagons bearing citizens and their belongings raced past, stopping only to let columns of cavalry and infantry march to war.

Drums beat as the armies of Demetia assembled along the northern sector.

"How long?" Megolin asked Clyde as he arrived beside the platform.

"They'll be here in five minutes," the general responded, watching the trebuchet crews load the arms with hay and stone, and pour buckets of tar on them.

Megolin turned to see Igraine watching from one of the buildings, a group of royal guards standing around her, their spears at the ready and two standard-bearers carrying their colors standing on either side.

Megolin galloped to the front of the line as the horns ceased.

"An army charges to attack us. But these are not the Highlanders. They may look like them, but they are not. Huns now thunder toward the enchanted forest, promising to lay waste to this land! Reports say eight thousand are approaching. We number five. But we are Demetians, and any race other than the Huns are fit to fight them. We will triumph, my brothers. And should we fall, we shall pass knowing that we defended our homeland!"

"Yah!" The soldiers shouted, beating their circle shields as they glared through their nasal helmets.

"Yah!" The cavalry boomed as they raised their spears.

King Megolin turned.

Silence descended on the city as they heard the sound of twenty thousand soldiers approaching.

Birds raced out of the trees as the armies drew near.

Megolin looked up and saw four fireballs streaking through the sky, trailing smoke.

"Launch!" An officer bellowed.

At once, the triggers were pulled and the arms released, catapulting a dozen stones of fire and hay balls of flame.

Horses reared and screamed as the cavalry and soldiers moved to avoid the incoming flames that crashed into the courtyard, sending burning chunks of hay flying out.

King Megolin saw the Demetian fireballs crash through canopy of the enchanted forest as he spotted Arthur leading his men toward the courtyard.

Looking to their right, he saw the Highlander army racing beside them, but could not recognize the commander who led the force.

Just then, the trebuchet crews launched another round of fireballs, and four more streaked toward the city guard northern barracks.

One of them hit a catapult as the twelve raced toward the enemy.

The trebuchet went up in flames, igniting the buckets of tar and the wagons carrying the stones and hay. The wreck of the catapult fell on the ground as the soldiers struggled to avoid it.

Flames raged across the cobblestone ground as Megolin saw the other end of the enchanted forest alight with fire.

Arthur emerged from the wood-line, his armor stained with blood, and Uther slumped unconscious behind him.

Merlin rode out behind him, and the two young men thundered to Megolin's side as the rest of the horses piled in. Magi Ro Hul raced toward them as the Highlanders charged behind.

"Your Grace," Arthur said, stopping by Megolin, "eight thousand soldiers and cavalry. But they are stronger than anticipated. Magi Ro Hul and I attacked them at a stream more than a dozen leagues north. We had to retreat."

Megolin looked at the Hun army advancing through the trees with calm.

Fires were burning behind him as officers shouted at their men to regroup.

"I need to get my father to safety," Arthur told the king.

"Verovingian!" Megolin called.

"I shall see it done, Arthur," he said, freeing Uther from the horse and carrying him away.

Another fireball streaked toward them, crashing into the roof of one of the city guard's barracks.

A fire erupted as the Demetian trebuchets returned fire.

The cavalry was reforming the line as the Huns thundered toward the courtyard.

"Spears!" General Clyde shouted, and the cavalry aimed their lances at the wood-line.

"Archers!" The general bellowed.

They held their arrows, their blades drenched with tar, to the torches before them.

"Draw!" A captain shouted.

"Loose!"

The shower of arrows raced up from the courtyard and the archers further back as the first line of Huns emerged from the trees.

Arthur drew his sword and raced toward them, slashing as the arrows fell on the ranks of Huns as they raced toward the cavalry.

"Charge!" Clyde bellowed as he struck a Hun soldier and the cavalry roared forward.

Crashing into the Hun line with their lances, they broke through the first ranks.

Arthur's sword rang loud against the steel of Bishkar's and the two men, with common blood, one wearing the armor of the other, dueled amidst the chaos of battle.

Arthur swung at him, only to miss as Bishkar jumped aside, his horse rearing.

Turning around, Arthur swung again, hitting Bishkar's sword.

Arrows raced past them as the Demetian and Highlander forces struggled to contain the Huns. But the enemy was spilling out into the rest of the northern sector.

Cutting down guards and infantry as they swarmed the dirt roads of the city, they broke into houses, looking for loot.

"Your father will not rejoin you," Bishkar taunted.

"You don't know my father," Arthur said, angrily, and lunged at the Hun general.

Bishkar jumped aside.

"It was my arrow, you know?"

Arthur stopped and stared at him.

Bishkar smiled.

"It was I who hit you with the arrow."

Arthur did not respond and charged at Bishkar.

Their swords collided as the two horses neighed.

Merlin was wielding a greatsword, the hilt carved out of oak. Cutting down Huns on either side of him, his blade merely incapacitated the men. Merlin never killed. He had sworn an oath not to, as all warlocks did. Their roles were to preserve life, not end it.

Not far from him, General Clyde was battling Hun cavalry as fireballs continued to streak across the sky and showers of arrows raced through the air.

The sound of battle echoed from throughout the northern sector as the Huns attacked the cavalry and infantry divisions protecting the city.

Fires erupted behind the courtyard as the expendables looted every building.

Arthur lunged at Bishkar, pushing him off his horse.

The Hun general fell to the cobblestone ground, his helmet clattering as it rolled off.

Arthur had landed on his side, his armor dented. He pushed himself up as Bishkar got back up.

He looked every bit the embodiment of the corruption and evil Rome had fallen into.

Arthur ran towards him, swinging his weapon with anger, hate, and pain.

The blade of his greatsword struck the Five Dragon crest of his own cuirass.

Over and over, he slashed at Bishkar, hitting the iron armor until it cracked.

Bishkar fell back, surprised at Arthur's string of attacks, but he quickly regained focus and jumped back up, slashing at Arthur. But Arthur parried the attacks.

Dodging every one, then parrying them, Bishkar soon grew enraged.

Silence passed between them as they battled, surrounded by soldiers on foot and horseback fighting to the death.

The trebuchets were no longer hurling fireballs through the air, but the enchanted forest was ablaze.

From a distance, Merlin harnessed the wind to direct the flames north, containing the fire, but that which was burning burned like Persepolis.

Bishkar was missing every time, while Arthur was hitting his mark.

Angry, Bishkar turned and pushed a Hun soldier off his horse while vaulting up himself. Thundering away from Arthur, his armor rent, he cut down Highlander and Demetian soldiers around him.

Arthur, tired by the duel, stood with his sword beside him, watching the battle. Horses were buckling as they fell to spears while cavalry fell off their horses. Arrows cut down soldiers while they ran, the fires from their blades engulfing them.

He turned and saw one of the streets leading to the rest of the city war-torn. Overturned wagons and fallen men and horses littered the road. Hun warriors battled the Demetians and Highlanders but were slowly being pushed back.

Arthur turned as he heard a Hun charging toward him, his ax held high and a voice shrieking from his throat.

Arthur slashed the man, felling him instantly. Then he turned to parry the blade of a Hun and drove his sword through the man's iron Highlander armor. The man fell to the ground.

Looking around, neither Megolin, Merlin, Magi Ro Hul, nor Clyde was anywhere to be seen.

Bodies littered the ground, many bristling with arrows. Horses struggled for breath as life slowly left them. Men were screaming from their wounds as the wrecks of the trebuchets burned. Pikes and lances whistled through the air, striking the horses of Demetian and Highlander cavalry.

But then a great horn echoed through the city.

"Stop!" Arthur heard Bishkar bellow, far louder than any human could possibly shout.

At once, the Huns stopped fighting, staring at their enemy with uncertainty.

"Fall back!" Bishkar commanded.

At once, the Hun expendables ran, pursued by Highlander and Demetian warriors.

Many were cut down as they disappeared amidst the trees again.

Arthur darted on foot, leading the charge through the enchanted forest.

Archers picked off retreating Huns as the rest of them ran, screaming and disorganized, around the great fire that burned.

Horses were galloping, some riderless.

Soon, Arthur, the Caledonians, and the Demetians emerged in the open.

Moon and starlight lit the grass where the light from the fires did not.

The Huns were howling, racing away from the capital of Demetia as Bishkar led the retreat.

Arthur returned to the courtyard.

Surviving soldiers walked amongst the fallen. No one was cheering. For every Hun that lay dead, five Demetians were lost forever. Fires still burned. The dais from which Megolin and Igraine had attended the departure of Arthur and Merlin, just that morning, was collapsed.

Arthur turned and saw Igraine standing with her royal guards. None of them had fallen, but they had cut down more than a hundred Huns.

Arthur, his brow bleeding and dotted with sweat, fell to the ground.

He heard the sound of a horse galloping and turned to see Merlin approaching.

"Ten thousand souls lost," he said. "Three thousand Demetians, two thousand Highlanders, and seven thousand Huns."

"Arthur," Megolin rode toward them. "Are you all right?"

Arthur nodded.

"Where's Magi Ro Hul?" he asked.

"He is approaching," Merlin announced, a moment later.

As he had foretold, the Caledonian general walked toward them.

An arrow protruded from his forearm.

He pulled it out as he walked over.

"Magi," Arthur said.

"Arthur."

"They will return," Megolin announced. "And this time, we will not be able to defend."

C.J. BROWN

7

IMPERIAL ASCENT

THE RIDER THUNDERED THROUGH THE gates of Rome, his uniform enough to let him through.

The hooves of his horse struck the cobblestone road as he galloped, headed for Palatine Hill.

Halting just outside the imperial palace, columns rising up before him, he jumped down and ran up the steps, past the Praetorian Guards who watched the entrance.

Bursting through the front doors, he raced toward the throne room, passing slaves, guards, and senators.

He pushed open the great doors of the emperor's throne room and heard the chatter between Lucius and Titus halt.

"Hail Ceasar!" He said, saluting the emperor.

"What news do you bring?" Lucius snarled, angry that his conversation had been broken.

"General Tiberius requests your permission to join the Hun invasion of Britannia. King Attila promises Rome will regain its former territory there. But Arthur and Uther are his, the Hun messenger said. Attila is setting out from Paris with war galleys, triremes and thousands of Huns, sire."

Lucius eyed the man for a moment.

"Yes," he muttered to himself. "I will help this fool. Then I will seize the accursed Pendragons from him and annihilate his foul race." He smiled.

"Tell General Tiberius that he may follow the Huns. Five thousand of our legionaries are worth more than a million Huns. Go."

The messenger struck his chest and turned to leave.

Lucius smiled.

Things were going better than he had hoped.

8

INVASION

SINCE THEY HAD OCCUPIED PARIS, the Frank galleys and triremes had been modified for better landing.

Ramps on either side of the bow would lower, allowing for most of the men to storm the beach while the rest jumped down from the deck. The galleys, with only a main deck, boasted ramps folded up at the bow, ready to be released.

Gerlach stood at the prow of the lead galley as the slaves rowed the ship along the Sequena, leading the column of triremes, war galleys, and other Frank ships.

Above, birds were circling, and along the banks, Franks watched as their enemy sailed to war.

The drums were beating as the trebuchets sat ready for deployment amongst the Hun warriors who sailed the ships making for the Narrow Sea.

Gerlach stared at the horizon with glee. Bred for war, peace was not what he desired. No, he had been trained to fight, to kill anyone who stood against him. His father, Adolphus, Attila, and the Hun king before this one had taught him that.

If not for power, just battle alone was enough for him.

The power of a hundred slaves rowing unceasingly, shouted at by Hun officers, and of the sails harnessing the wind, sent the ships toward the channel at a steady pace of ten knots.

Wakes drew from the prows of the galleys and triremes.

Forty thousand men, overcrowded and crammed into fewer than thirty ships, were ready for war.

Gerlach knew his plan. He would land along the southern coast of Britannia, while the ships from Le Havre would land along the eastern shore and at Dornoch.

From there, they would attack every kingdom, every tribe, every city. Only Arthur, Uther, and the Caledonians would be spared, the former to be captured and sent back to Attila.

Within an hour, they were reaching the Narrow Sea and Gerlach looked out at the water.

He could not see Britannia yet.

Less than an hour later, Gerlach turned to see a fleet of thirty galleys and triremes charging to join him, carrying ten thousand Huns. Gerlach smiled at the prospect that his army would soon number fifty. The plans that were hatched earlier were falling into place nicely. The new recruits were also deployed, and the Hun's strength had all but fully returned.

He turned back to the isle as the galley heaved on the Narrow Sea, moving fast by the power of the oars and the wind.

The sun was sinking lower in the sky and the shadows grew long by the time the Huns could see the plains and trees of Britannia. The thirty galleys and triremes had disappeared from sight again, and the main fleet was within trebuchet range of the shore.

Torches burned at the bows and sterns of the ships as they rowed towards the beach.

Gerlach, already acclimated to the darkness, stared at the coast.

He snarled when he saw a lone rider watch the ships approach, then turn and head north.

"Never mind," he said to himself.

"Prepare to land!" He boomed.

"Ramp crews, be ready!" The captain shouted as the captain of the company aboard the flagship ordered his men to attention.

Commotion sounded behind him as they prepared.

Ramps meant for the trebuchets were being readied as the galley reached the shore.

Men fell to the deck as the ship crashed into the sand.

Gerlach held his stand and jumped down from the ship as the rest of his men recovered themselves.

Along the beach, the rest of the triremes, galleys, and vessels were landing.

Soldiers began storming out of holds and off the decks as they raced up the beach.

The men of Gerlach's ship streamed from the deck, and Gerlach watched as thirty thousand Huns stormed the shore of Britannia, the rest landing at the eastern shore.

9

ALLIANCE OF HATE

KING FERGUS SAT SILENTLY IN his court. The fire crackled in its hearth while the twelve members of the War Council looked at him.

"War with Demetia has restarted," he said. "But we do not fight the Demetians. We fight only one man. Arthur. Because of him, my daughter is gone. Because of him, my family is gone. Gallagher will be the one to succeed me, but so my line has ended. We will try to offer terms of peace to the Demetians to surrender Arthur."

"I'm sorry, Your Grace," Jon responded, "but the Demetians will not agree to any terms if that is the condition. They are an honorable people. They will not give up a friend."

"But they risk years of war," Fergus said.

"That will not deter them," the Prime Minister offered.

King Fergus grew irritated.

"Never mind," he growled. "Lord Uther will be king of the neutral land. Then the Demetians will have no way to win. We will squash them like a roach."

The room stayed silent, the Council's ultimate form of protest, second to treason.

"Yes," Fergus said, "we will crush the Demetians."

The sound of iron on iron echoed from outside when the great doors creaked open.

"Gallagher," Fergus said, rising. "What news?"

The heir to Caledonia and the Roman Empire looked at Fergus.

"Magi Ro Hul has betrayed us."

"What?" Fergus bellowed, rising from his throne.

"He attacked us when we stopped to drink and water our horses. Then Arthur appeared with Demetian cavalry. But we were able to rout them and fought them at Demetia."

Fergus' eyes flared with rage.

"And Arthur?"

"Forgive me, Your Grace, but we had to retreat. We did not apprehend the fool."

Fergus stared at Gallagher.

"You dare to let go the man who caused my daughter's death?" He bellowed.

"I'm sorry, Your Grace," Gallagher replied, hiding

the irritation he felt for Fergus, "but we were battling two fierce armies."

"Fiercer than those accursed Huns?"

Gallagher felt his anger rising when Fergus insulted his people, adopted though they may be. He did not respond.

"How many losses?"

"Seven thousand, Your Grace."

"Worthless Huns!" The king bellowed.

"We will win next time," Gallagher said.

"You should hope so," Fergus said, poison dripping from his words. "Or I will see your head beside Arthur's. Capture Magi Ro Hul along with the Roman."

Gallagher nodded, and turned, leaving Fergus to fume.

C.J. BROWN

10

UNITING A KINGDOM

ARTHUR STORMED INTO KING MEGOLIN'S great hall.

Magi Ro Hul was there, along with Merlin, Clyde, Igraine, Megolin, and other members of the king's court.

The ministers were filling in as Arthur ascended the dais and stood by his cousin.

A Demetian messenger stood to the right of the group of ministers.

"This meeting has been called for an unprecedented threat now stands before us," Megolin said, his voice grim. The air of the great hall was sour with grief and anger.

"Seventy thousand Huns have landed along our shores."

Arthur lost all expression as the hall erupted in shouts of disbelief. He realized that the Huns had recruited their numbers from the Ostrogoths ahead of arriving on the isles. Attila's ability to raise his forces was well known across Europe.

"Silence!" Megolin boomed.

Quiet returned.

"Even now, towns and cities have most likely already fallen to them. Even now, they march on Demetia. Soon the reports of raging fires, cities turned to ash, and green fields turned to wastelands will arrive. By then, it will be too late. I fear it already is."

He paused.

"Magi Ro Hul, a fine man, promises that the armies of Caledonia are loyal no longer to Fergus, but to sense, and to our cause. Still, the Highlanders and we will not be able to defend against the actions of a deranged king and seventy thousand barbarians who decimate our lands as we speak. As it is, their foul faces are seen across the continent. Now they promise to shroud the land with their darkness.

"We must find some way to defeat them. Gallagher is a Hun. He has paved the way for this to happen."

The king seated himself, while his ministers, generals, and advisors processed the information they had just learned, the darkest of all. Arthur was contemplating the situation.

There seemed to be almost no hope.

"We could flee," one of the ministers said.

Enraged, Megolin turned and jumped up. "Cowardice is not something that will be tolerated here! Either we fight and win, or we die fighting!"

Magi Ro Hul eyed the king as the rest of them did. He decided Megolin was more worthy of the Caledonian throne than Fergus ever was. If Fergus was able to turn to darkness now, he was never truly wise.

Arthur thought back to everything he knew about Britannia, everything his father had taught him about warfare, about facing grim odds.

His thoughts led him to realize that disunity had been the cause of all this chaos, all this destruction. "What about the other fourteen tribes?" He said.

The chatter of the ministers, generals, and advisors stopped.

"What do you mean?" Clyde asked.

Arthur knew what he was about to suggest would seem impossible. It was the second time he was thinking it. Perhaps he'd have a better plan now.

"What if we all united? Fifteen tribes, hopefully Caledonia as well, band together to defeat the Huns."

"What you are suggesting Arthur, has not been able to be accomplished by any king for centuries."

"Yes, Your Grace, but perhaps this will make the lords of Britannia see reason."

King Fergus eyed him silently.

"Your suggestion will be considered, Arthur. But elaborate first."

"I will be honest," Arthur responded, "I know nothing of Britannia, other than it is divided by sixteen tribes who have remained peaceful for fifty years. Good relations, I hope, are maintained with them. But regardless, the threat of an invasion by the worst people known to man should turn even Fergus back to reason. I will speak with them. Send emissaries too, for we do not have time."

"It's worth an attempt," Magi Ro Hul said.

"Relations are acceptable with the other fourteen tribes," Megolin said. "The closest is Rodwin. Lord Lancelot rules there. He is just, wise, and will be willing to listen."

"Then I shall meet with him first," Arthur said.

The doors opened as the court considered Arthur's suggestion.

It was not something to just accept or disagree with immediately.

"Lord Arthur," a royal guard announced, "your father has awoken."

Arthur looked at him as the hall fell silent. He had told the guard assigned to watch over his chambers to alert him as soon as Uther woke up. He had not fully prepared what he was going to say yet.

"Forgive me, Your Grace. Ministers," he said. "I must leave."

Megolin nodded.

Arthur turned and headed towards the doors, with the royal guard beside him. His steps almost sounded like far-off thuds to him as he focused his mind and heart. He remembered what Merlin told him about his father, and what his mother had said.

He hoped he would be able to return his father to himself.

Emerging from the king's court, he saw soldiers clearing the roads. Horses and men were being carried away on wagons. Merlin had put out the fire of the enchanted wood the night before. Dawn did not arrive with any less grief, for mourning could be heard from every corner of the city. Civilians had returned to their homes where the Huns had attacked, only to find them burnt.

Soldiers still littered the courtyard, but they were being cleared as buckets of water were used to wash away the blood.

The smell of ash still lingered as Arthur followed the royal guard to the palace.

His cloak flowing behind him, Arthur walked without armor as a cool breeze raced along the road. His tunic flowing in the wind, they reached the palace doors and entered.

The royal guard led Arthur up to the third level and

they stopped before great wooden doors at a corner, sconces lighting up the corridors.

The guard returned to his post by the door, the other having stood watch while he left to call Arthur.

The former heir to the Pendragon clan stood before the doors, silent.

His eyes appeared to drift as he stared at the engraved oak. He felt lost, for one of the few times in his life.

He opened the door and walked in. Uther was standing by the window. All weapons, all candles, all things that could possibly be used to harm had been cleared from the room. Arthur had ordered that himself. He knew what state his father was in.

Uther did not turn at the sound of someone entering.

Outside, horses were neighing as they pulled wagons of fallen soldiers to be buried while other soldiers cleaned the streets of blood and weapons.

"Father," Arthur began, and Uther spun around to see his son.

"You!" He bellowed.

Arthur did not want to respond with anger.

"Father, please, listen to me—"

"First, you insult me, then you betray me. You have renounced your Pendragon name. You are no longer my son. You are my enemy!"

Uther lunged at him, but Arthur jumped aside.

"Father, you are in pain."

"You know nothing of pain," Uther growled.

Arthur stood still, the wound of losing Olivie still fresh for him.

"I do know," he said, looking away.

He noticed Uther's face change. For a moment, he looked at his son without anger or malice, but with sorrow.

But the moment of lucidity evaporated as quickly as it arrived.

"You do not know the things I have had to do," Uther said. "My father treated me like a slave. He ordered me to slay my son and the one I loved, or I would not be emperor."

"You were bound by greed," Arthur said.

"Greed?" Uther shouted, mad with rage.

"You regarded the throne with greater importance than your own family. And now you seek to make things right by helping your son, no matter what he is."

"You think you know me," Uther said. "You are mistaken. I am a Roman. You are nothing like it."

Arthur paused, feeling lost.

"No," he said. "I am not a Roman. The golden age of Rome has long since passed. Now, all that remains is the corruption, evil, and greed of unworthy emperors."

"You dare insult your people?" Uther bellowed. "The emperors?"

"No," Arthur said. "I speak only the truth. You saw it before. You were going to change things."

Uther looked like a mad dog about to attack.

"Rome is greatest. I am its emperor, and so it shall be a city of the gods."

"Father, you must see reason," Arthur responded, abandoning the debate about Rome. "Bulanid is not your son. He never was. He never knew you. He never learned from you. He was never with you. But I was. You taught me everything I know, you and Mother. You may have loved another before, but then you grew to love Mother, and if you only give life a chance, you will see that you can right your wrongs with your family, with your new life. Gallagher is not your son. His fate is not in your hands. He doesn't love you."

Uther paused.

"Where is he?"

"Gone," Arthur said. "He retreated with his Huns. He's a Hun general, Father."

"My own flesh and blood leading the enemy," Uther said.

"He may be your flesh and blood, but he is nothing like you. I am. I do not want the throne. I do not even want to be heir. All I'm asking for is for the man who taught me that honor was the greatest principle, that family was the only truly important thing. And family goes beyond blood. One may be a parent, or a child, but still not be family if one does not care for other family members, or does not see family for almost forty years, at the start of which one was but a child."

Uther remained silent, his face showing the grief and anger he harbored.

Arthur could feel it.

"As we speak, seventy thousand Huns are attacking this land. They landed last night. They will lay waste to the isle. They will burn cities to the ground. Slaves will grow their army. If we do not stand together, there is no hope. If King Fergus remains lost, there is no hope. Unity, Father, is what makes a people survive. But once they are fighting each other, any chance of defeating a greater peril is lost. So, even if only for the good of the world, I beseech you, put aside your pain, and march with me."

Uther stared at him.

"Lies!" He shouted. "You say this only to trick me. But it will not work."

Arthur closed his eyes as a tear rolled down his cheek.

"I'm sorry, Father," Arthur said, and turned to leave.

"Fool!" He shouted. "My son will return. He will free me from this prison! You will fall. This accursed kingdom will fall!"

Arthur stormed out of the room and headed towards the stairwell. Rushing toward the front doors, he burst out of the palace within minutes.

Running down the oaken steps, he almost collapsed as he struggled to regain his senses. He was losing his father more day by day. Arthur did not know what to do.

"Do not relent," he heard Merlin say. "He is Uther, father of Arthur. He will not abandon you."

Arthur cried at Merlin's words, unable to see.

"How?" He said.

"Be his son."

Arthur's eyes opened.

Wiping away his tears, he stood back up, and walked back to the great hall, where he had first met King Megolin a lifetime ago.

As he walked toward his seat, Megolin rose.

"Arthur," he said, "your suggestion is wise. There isn't much time, so you will depart for Rodwin as soon as possible. We will send emissaries to the other lands as well. Travel light. A small contingent of fifty men will go with you."

Arthur hid the pain of the conversation he had just had with his father.

"Yes, Your Grace. I shall leave at once."

Within moments, Arthur was donning his armor.

He had cleaned it the night before. His sharpened sword sat on the great oak table by his bed.

With all but his helmet fitted, he buckled his sword and walked out with his great normar on his mop of black hair.

His Demetian cloak flowing behind him, he walked to his horse, handled by Verovingian.

"Friend," he said, "Gaea has something planned for you. I know not what it is, but it is something great."

Arthur looked at his friend, puzzled.

"How do you know?"

"When you are connected with nature, with the way of things, what will happen appears easily to you."

Arthur nodded. "Thank you, my friend."

Verovingian smiled.

Arthur vaulted up onto his horse and raised his hand to Verovingian.

Pulling the reins, he galloped toward the spot where he had seen the people of Demetia assemble to greet him, when he first arrived the day they landed at Inver Ridge.

Trumpets were blaring from the city guard posts as fifty cavalrymen began following Arthur. Carrying pennons and a banner, the Demetians formed up before him. Emissaries were preparing beside him, all leading contingents of fifty horses. They would set out for the rest of the tribes and kingdoms.

The sound of hooves striking the dried leaves and dirt rang loud as Arthur eyed his men.

"We travel north, to Rodwin," he said, "to seek an audience with Lord Lancelot. We go there in peace. Only should we see the Huns do we draw our swords."

"Yes, my lord," they said.

Arthur, his face cold, turned his horse around.

Breaking into a gallop he charged amidst the trees, his horse jumping over fallen barks as it raced.

Behind, fifty horses thundered after him, charging through the ash that still drifted through the air.

C.J. BROWN

11

DARKNESS RISING

THE EXPENDABLES ROARED ACROSS THE plains as the Hun cavalry charged from behind.

Arrows flew up from the streets of Egolith, the Demetian city closest to the shore.

Trebuchets hurled stones and fireballs that trailed smoke and streaked through the dawn air as the expendables collided with the lances of the cavalry who stood guard by the main gate.

Gerlach watched from the ridge as twenty thousand Franks battled the Demetian cavalry and infantry.

Line upon line of expendables were falling to the will of the Demetian warriors and Gerlach grew angry.

He hadn't been expecting such strong resistance.

But he would soon unleash the true force of the Hun empire, and the cities of Demetia would crumble.

***

He slashed at a Frankish fellow, clad in Hun colors, as he struggled to hold the line.

"Stay together, men!" The commander bellowed.

He looked up and saw a fireball streaking toward them.

It crashed just yards away, sending chunks of burning hay flying toward them.

Horses reared as the men struggled to hold their place.

"Archers!" Captain Simron shouted, and at once another arrow raced up into the air. Simron was a man of few words, but when he shouted, hundreds fell to his command.

Smoke spiraled up amidst the fog as the wood-line burned, set alight by flame hurled up by Demetian catapults.

From all around, the Huns were charging toward the city.

Axes, swords, and spears crashed against the circle shields of the Demetian cavalry.

Simron raised his shield and pushed aside a Hun sword. Then he cut the Hun down with his own blade and turned to slash at another attacking his brethren just to his left.

"Left flank!" The resolute captain shouted.

Simron turned and saw a mass of Huns thundering toward them from the east.

At once, the line of horses forming the left side of the phalanx turned and aimed their lances at the enemy.

"Right flank!"

At once, Simron turned, his sword shining from the fires that burned around them.

"Hold the line!"

Simron stared through his nasal helmet at the Huns as they ran, an army of darkness, of all things reviled.

The sound of their shrieks and their stomps echoed across the burning plains of Egolith when Simron raised his sword, and they ran through the cavalry phalanx just ahead. He cut down the first Hun that crashed into them.

Simron struck Hun after Hun till his arm burned. His shield bristled with arrows as the ranks of the enemy appeared before them like the Persian Immortals who defeated the Spartans at the Battle of Thermopylae.

As he slashed around his horse, a stone flew through the air and struck the wall above them.

Shouts rang out as guards atop the parapets fell with the stones. One of the watchtowers collapsed, crushing a number of the warriors behind Simron.

The Demetian banner fell to the ground as the Huns redoubled the attack.

Around him, his brothers fell, their horses rearing in pain as the Huns sent them retreating over the fallen rocks.

Simron thundered into the city and watched as the Huns poured in.

He was slashing at one of them when a spear hit his horse.

It reared, throwing him off.

Landing on the dirt road, he jumped up as the horse fell to the ground.

Fighting on foot, he parried every blow and cut down Huns as they flooded the city.

A few cavalrymen still fought with him, while the remaining phalanxes were being sent retreating back through the gates.

Archers picked off Huns from the remaining watchtowers and the buildings, but fire and stone crashed into the houses and shops. Hun arrows took out the soldiers as Simron fought, his shield before him.

Then an arrow hit his chest.

He stumbled back, blood leaking from his lungs as they flooded.

Dazed, and struggling to breathe, he lunged at a Hun soldier, cutting him down, when another arrow hit him. Bristling from his shoulder, he dropped his shield and fell to his knees.

Slashing Huns as they ran around him, he was hit with another arrow, then another.

Coughing up blood, he swung his blade at one of the barbarians.

His vision growing blurry, and his lungs struggling to breathe, his eyes darted back and forth as the Huns raced through the city. Buildings were engulfed in flame as the enemy carried off gold and silver.

A blade slashed Simron's chest, and he fell back, his eyes staring blankly at the sky.

C.J. BROWN

12

THE EAGLE HAS LANDED

TIBERIUS LED HIS LEGION THROUGH the streets of Paris, the first Roman general to walk the city in decades.

The banner of Rome was looked on with disgust by the Franks and Huns alike, and Tiberius could feel their hatred.

He didn't care. He would be the emperor's greatest general. Perhaps Lucius would appoint him heir, endowing him with the greatest power. As emperor, Tiberius would grow the Roman Empire more than any of his predecessors had. He would see Roman garrisons as far as the uncharted west. He would occupy all of Britannia, the cold lands to the north. Rome would be the greatest city for the rest of time.

The legionnaires of Chimaerum marched with discipline. The horses of the cavalry neighed as they traversed the cobblestone road.

A line of war galleys was awaiting them at the Sequena, along with Hun captains and slaves.

Tiberius stopped before the gangplank of the first galley. "Make haste!" he shouted. "We leave at once."

"Move!" A Hun captain bellowed.

At once the legionnaires marched with their shields over the gangplank. Filing onto the deck, five hundred of them took their place while the rest boarded the remaining ships. Tiberius would have preferred they were all galleys, but there hadn't been enough time to build them. They'd have to make do with merchant ships, boats, and other vessels.

Once the legionaries and the cavalry had boarded the ships, around the trebuchets that each galley carried, Tiberius turned, not looking at the Hun captain who stood beside him and galloped onto the deck.

Jumping down, he landed with a thud as the Hun captain raced aboard and shouts were bellowed to remove the gangplanks.

Tiberius looked north.

He could not see the Narrow Sea, though he could in his mind.

He envisioned a grand campaign. He would use the

Huns, see them capture Arthur and Uther, then seize them and defeat the barbarians. Lucius would appoint him as heir.

Smirking, he heard the captain shout for the sails to be deployed and for the slaves to start rowing.

Men, broken by evil, propelled the ships out to sea amidst dawn air, just two days since the Hun messenger had forwarded Attila's proposal. The Roman rider had returned, fatigued with travel, only to pass on the answer of the emperor and fall unconscious.

He was left to the care of the Franks.

Less than three hours later, a storm was brewing over the Narrow Sea as the galleys and triremes heaved.

Tiberius looked around to see some of the boats drifting away uncontrollably while the smaller ones sank. Only the galleys and triremes made it safely to the shore.

As rain pelted the sails and the deck, the galley halted suddenly, amongst the Hun ships that had sailed for Britannia two days past.

High tide sent waves that destabilized the Hun triremes and galleys.

"Debark!" The Hun captain bellowed over the storm.

Tiberius gave no counter-order, and so the legionnaires streamed from the decks as the cavalry thundered off.

They raced up the beach as lightning clapped above. Tiberius jumped from the deck with his horse and thundered up to the rocks.

"March!" He shouted, as the legion assembled, and the horses formed their ranks around them.

Drawing his sword, he turned and strode towards the forest, leading the cohorts off the beach, and marching on the lands of Britannia, the first such legion in centuries.

13

SPUTTERING ALLIANCES

ARTHUR AND HIS CONTINGENT OF fifty riders approached the walls of Rodwin as the sun shone from high above.

Archers could be seen lining the parapets, but none of them were aiming arrows at the Demetians.

The banner of a wreath hung above the main gate.

Arthur stopped a stone's throw from the raised drawbridge.

"We arrive in peace," Arthur bellowed at the commander above the gate.

"Clearly," he said. "Or else you'd be dead by now."

Silence grew as Arthur watched the wall and the Demetian banner flew in the wind.

"I do not recognize you," the man said.

"I am Arthur. I am not of this land," the general responded.

"What's your clan?"

Arthur lost his thought for a moment, his brow losing its structure at the question that almost sent the blood draining from his head.

"I have no family," he said, painfully.

The man of Rodwin looked at Arthur with pity.

"Let them through!" he ordered.

Arthur looked to see the drawbridge lower across the moat, filled with tar and bristling with spikes.

The portcullis creaked as it rose upward, behind which the same man he had just spoken to appeared, and Arthur strode forward, leading the Demetian cavalry to the gate.

They rode through the gate, amassing by the wall as the drawbridge was raised and the portcullis lowered.

"Normally, the city is free for travelers," the man said, "but we know what has taken place recently. The isle is no longer safe."

Arthur nodded.

"I am the guardian of these borders," the man said, to Arthur's surprise. "State your purpose."

"Lord Lancelot," Arthur said, jumping down from his horse. "The isle is about to be overrun by Huns. King Fergus has already allied with them, though he does not know it. The Highlander army has joined us, but Fergus will not relent. There is one named Bulanid Mehmet, or

Gallagher. He has turned the Caledonian king against the Demetians, myself, and any who stand against him. If he continues fighting this war, there is no hope of defeating the barbarians."

Lancelot eyed him carefully.

Arthur was not lying. But what was he asking?

"If you are requesting our help, I'm sorry, but we cannot. We have hardly enough men to defend our borders from possible threats of the isle. Now that Fergus has gone mad, we must be ready to fight the Highlanders. We cannot fight the Huns as well. Let's speak in the great hall."

"No, there is no time," Arthur said urgently.

Lancelot nodded.

"Emissaries have been sent to the other fourteen tribes and kingdoms. It is the will of Demetia, for the good of the isle and all who live here that we band together to defeat the sixty-thousand strong Huns who remain on our shores. Turn Fergus back to reason, somehow, but we must unite, or else all is lost."

"The Huns are a despicable race. There is no doubt about that," Lancelot answered, thoughtfully. "They overrun Roman legions. There's a good chance they've defeated the Franks too."

"That's true," Arthur said.

Lancelot's face turned grim.

"The Franks are the greatest fighting force the continent has seen, second to the Romans. The Huns are stronger than both because of their brutality, their barbaric ways, and their unmatched numbers. When they were first at their strongest, they commanded almost a million men, threatening Gaul's borders and Italy itself. They were defeated only by the actions of a wise emperor. But long has it been since the Empire was ruled by someone worthy. Now, with almost sixty thousand warriors, they storm the isle. If there is no hope, we can only flee."

"To where?" Arthur said, not trying to be sarcastic.

"The great ocean is not the end of the world," Lancelot said. "There must be something there for the people of this isle, and for any who may escape the rule of the Huns."

"We must fight," Arthur repeated.

"I'm sorry, Arthur," Lancelot said.

Arthur looked at the lord of Rodwin with anger and fear.

"Then perhaps the people of Britannia will find hope elsewhere."

Vaulting up onto his horse, he heard Lancelot then order the guards to raise the gate and lower the drawbridge.

Arthur watched the iron gate creak upward, anger and sorrow burdening his mind and heart.

Once the portcullis was just above the height of a spear held by a cavalry warrior, Arthur broke into a gallop and thundered out, followed by the Demetian riders.

Lancelot watched the Demetian envoy leave, his heart and mind heavy.

Arthur raced silently back to Demetia.

Along the way, other Demetian riders were seen racing

back to the city, envoys returning from the kingdoms closest to Megolin's.

Arthur feared they too had failed.

An hour before sunset, three of the envoys who had departed Demetia thundered to a halt within the city.

King Megolin was there, as was Igraine and Merlin. Magi Ro Hul stood by them as they watched Arthur and the other emissaries stream into the city. Buildings still lay crumbled and burned, but the rest had been cleared.

"Your Grace," Arthur said, "Lancelot will not join us."

"Nor will Gawain, Your Grace," another said, bowing before Megolin.

"Or Galahad."

"Neither will Geraint."

Megolin looked solemn, as did Merlin.

Igraine was pondering the implications of this failure and remaining strong amidst her family.

"Lord Lancelot says they do not have enough men, that they will flee if they must, but now they must defend against the threat of Fergus."

"Lord Geraint said that his people do not want war. They too will flee if there is no other choice, but they will not fight. Centuries of war have taught them that peace, no matter what, is worth more than anything."

"But there shall be no peace when evil rules the world," Arthur objected.

"And Galahad hopes that he might strike a deal with the Huns. Anything to survive without war."

"Let us speak to them again, Father," Merlin said. "I can show them what even we have not seen with our own eyes. A Roman legion will land at the coast two days hence. The city of Egolith has fallen, overrun by Huns."

Arthur straightened at the news.

"Be strong, my son," Igraine said. "You must not let fear cloud your judgment."

Arthur nodded.

"How is Father?"

"He has not sent for anyone. He is resting."

Igraine did not want to tell her son that the guards had heard him muttering to himself, sounding like a madman as he roamed the almost empty wooden room.

"Rest. Break bread. Then head back out. The Huns will be here within the week," Megolin said.

An hour later, Arthur was finishing his meat and cheese with Magi Ro Hul, the first Highlander to ever sit at the Demetian royal table.

Then he donned his helmet, said farewell to the king and his mother, then left with Merlin and fifty riders.

Charging out of the forest, they headed straight for Rodwin.

14

ENEMIES ALIGNED

BISHKAR WATCHED THE SHIPS APPROACH, the evening breeze drifting over the rocks.

A few wharves, meant to host the ships of the Caledonian fleet that numbered only ten galleys, were not enough for the forty ships that now charged toward the coast, while the other twenty landed at Demetia's eastern shore.

King Fergus watched from his horse as the Hun force approached.

"I will confess," Gallagher began, "I am also Hun."

"What?" Fergus boomed, before an army of three thousand royal guards.

"Yes, but I do not seek to occupy your kingdom, nor

does King Attila. We only wish to vanquish Arthur and Uther. Demetia will fall. Every kingdom here but yours will fall. You may claim any you wish, but the land Rome once occupied will be returned to them. Only Arthur and Uther are Attila's."

Fergus eyed Gallagher with anger.

"It was your arrow that hit Arthur and my daughter," Fergus said. "Do not test my restraint further."

Gallagher eyed Fergus carefully.

He was treading on thin ice. He had already angered the king more than any other. There couldn't be any more surprises.

Moonlight shone off the waves as they crashed against the rocks and the ships approached the only safe harbor.

The first galley, bristling with hundreds of Huns, halted by the first quay, shouts sounding from the deck. As they began to debark, other galleys and triremes planted their oars by the wharves, and barbarians began streaming off. Further out, the bulk of the fleet halted beyond the dock.

Huns waded through the frigid water as King Fergus watched the barbarians begin to walk up the path to the green fields, within sight of where Gallagher had cut down a thousand Huns and their commander.

The horses neighed at the smell of the Huns reaching them. With their chipped blades and hodge-podge shields, the barbarian army of twenty thousand ascended the rocks.

The royal guard immediately encircled the king, while the bulk of the three thousand cleared a path for the Huns.

Rows of three, stretching from the dock, where Highlander guards and soldiers watched the Huns with anger, streamed past the king.

"They will be commanded by General Gerlach," Gallagher said, looking through spears and lances that passed between them. "He leads the force that is currently attacking Demetia. This group will attack from the north, while the other ten thousand attack from the east coast, leaving nowhere to run. I request a camp outside Pittentrail to host five thousand of these men, as a garrison. The rest will begin the campaign at dawn."

King Fergus eyed him quietly, fog drifting around him.

"Should any of them appear to harbor hostile intentions against my people," he said, calmly, "none of them will be spared."

Gallagher nodded. He knew what the Highlanders could do. This wasn't an empty threat.

"The other kingdoms of the isle will most likely stand against you, Your Grace," Gallagher said. "I suggest we attack them first."

"Very well," Fergus responded. "Of the fifteen tribes, Caledonia shall claim three. You may keep the rest. I hope to negotiate with the emperor about Demetia, though, for that land is a realm my fathers have desired since the days of The Great War. It is not something I, nor my people, can let go."

"I fear you will find no success there," Gallagher argued, enraging the Highlander king. "Emperor Lucius is greedy for power. He will not easily give up land, especially that which he was promised."

"Then I will fight him for it."

Gallagher eyed the king, then turned back to watch the rest of the Huns stream from the ships.

A few hours later, the Huns were setting up camp outside Pittentrail.

Campfires lit up the walls of the city as the guards assembled, training arrows at the foul allies. King Fergus was not going to leave anything to chance.

Gallagher eyed the archers atop the wall as the men sat by their fires, roasting meat and drinking mead. Laughter sounded from the camp as the men talked of the war ahead.

Gallagher, alone, sat astride his destrier near the main gate, where Arthur had escaped with Olivie less than a week past.

The warmth of the campfires could be felt from where he watched.

But hatred and anger proved the greater fires that warmed him that the cold night, with winter approaching. He thought of Uther, and the pain he had caused him, of Attila and the kindness he had shown him. Attila had been more a father to him than any man had ever been, but for the Anatolian husband his mother had wed after Uther left, Bishkar surmised, only to return to slay his own son.

Bishkar found himself raging with bile and anger when the gate opened.

Shaken out of his thoughts, he turned and saw a captain leading men carrying shovels and equipment.

"Move!" he shouted. "There is much work to do!"

Horses neighed as they dragged wagons bearing wooden planks and logs.

Gallagher realized they were building a trench system for the five thousand Huns.

It was a good idea. They would be safe and would be able to repel any attack that was launched against Pittentrail.

Near the camp, the trebuchet crews were lining the catapults behind the tent city, with the wagons of stone and tar by their side.

The horses were encircled by wood and rope that formed makeshift barriers.

The smell of food drifted up from the camp, while the city guard watched.

C.J. BROWN

15

THE VISION

FIFTY-TWO RIDERS APPROACHED THE GATES of Rodwin.

The guard keeping a watchful eye on the plains around the city recognized the Demetian banner and sent for Lord Lancelot.

Arthur stopped once again before the moat, his horse neighing.

The Demetian cavalry stopped behind him, their beasts rearing and snickering.

The Demetian banner and pennons streamed in the cold breeze that rolled across the grass. Winter was near, and with it, the nights were growing cold and merciless.

"Let them through!" The captain of the guard ordered,

eyeing the yellow eyes and glowing robes of the rider beside Arthur.

At once, the drawbridge lowered, and the portcullis creaked as it rose.

Arthur strode through the gate and stopped in the courtyard as the rest of the riders followed.

Their hooves striking the dirt road, the city's garrison stood silent around the Demetian envoy.

All of them had heard the conversation between him and Lord Lancelot earlier that day.

Since then, guards had shifted their feet more often. When their shifts ended, they hurried to their homes. The fires of the watchtowers were kept raging, and archers were on guard.

The cavalry was ready to assemble at a moment's notice, and the soldiers were restless, unable to eat, with their swords beside them.

"Lord Lancelot will meet you in the great hall," the captain of the Lord's Guard said.

"Leave your horses here and follow me."

Arthur nodded to the Demetians and got down from his horse.

A number of guards approached them to lead their horses away.

In silence, Arthur, Merlin, and the fifty soldiers followed the captain of the Lord's Guard.

Passing the stone and wooden buildings, they walked

the dirt road, passing a tavern from which no laughs were heard, homes where civilians kept their windows closed.

Arthur, with his greatsword at his side, marched beside Merlin, whose cloak, glowing blue, swept the street.

Within half an hour, Arthur spotted the great hall, a humble stone building rising three levels. Four towers rose like spires from the corners of the building, where guards watched the city and the fields beyond, great fires raging before them, like the eternal flame of the gods from which Prometheus had stolen to bless mankind with light and warmth.

Two of the guards at the great hall nodded and turned to raise the iron bar that kept the doors shut.

Pushing them open, a long corridor was revealed. The aisle leading to Lord Lancelot's seat was decorated with red and gold carpet. Benches sat on either side of the aisle, like the pews of a church. The banner of the lords of Rodwin hung from anchors along the walls. Like great curtains, they lay still, flanked by torches that burned steadily.

A great fire raged to warm the hall, the steps of Arthur and Merlin almost quiet as they walked over the rich carpet.

"You remain outside," the captain said to the fifty riders.

Arthur turned and nodded.

The first Demetian rider who had stepped in walked back out and the great doors were shut.

Two more guards stood by the doors inside, eyeing the visitors.

Arthur nodded at Merlin and turned to see Lord Lancelot rise from his seat.

"You seek an audience for the second time this day. Pray tell, why do you return to a place where you will not find what you are looking for?"

"I am Merlin, son of King Megolin," the warlock said, bowing before the lord of Rodwin.

"And what business brings the heir to the throne of Demetia hither?" Lancelot asked, still standing amidst the empty chairs of his court.

"I have seen what the Huns have already done to the isle, and what will come to pass should they succeed. I wish to show it to you."

Lancelot eyed him suspiciously.

All beyond the borders of Demetia were unbelieving of the magic its people wielded, and of the ability of those who just believed in it.

Arthur remembered he once stood where Lancelot now did, not understanding the abilities of some.

"Very well," Lancelot said.

Merlin closed his eyes.

Arthur watched as the warlock did nothing.

But then Lancelot stumbled back, his eyes white and glowing.

Shrouded in light, he saw Hun armies thundering through the city of Egolith, a bustling trade city where merchants and traders from the continent regularly traded along the Blue Stream. Fires raged. A Hun slashed a man running from the barbaric horde.

Suddenly, the vision switched to a land burning with flame, the green fields turned to wastelands, the Hun armies marching, the drums beating, against the city of Demetia, the enchanted wood ablaze, the city in ruins, of Pittentrail falling to darkness, of slaves shackled to oars and standing by furnaces, fashioning weapons of war.

Arthur was watching it too, his heart racing. Suddenly, the vision turned to a flash of light and both he and Lancelot stumbled back, falling to the ground.

Arthur, ten yards from the lord of Rodwin, sat on the carpet, breathing fast, like when he had awoken from that dream the morning he defeated Adolphus' men within range of the Alps.

Lancelot was recovering from his fall, his eyes closed.

"That is what shall be should the Huns triumph. The rule of the Romans, as insufferable as it was, will be nothing compared to the tyranny of the Huns. The vile Attila will see this land turned to ash. He promises the land Rome once held returned to them, but he is not a man honor. No corner of the isle will be safe. And with the power the Huns will have, no corner of the continent."

Lancelot fell into the throne of his father, his grandfather, and his ancestors of old, the eyes of the first lord of Rodwin, staring above him from the painting that hung above and behind.

Arthur stood back up, his mind almost distant.

"My people will flee," Lancelot said, to Merlin and Arthur's dismay. "We have but five thousand warriors, far less than what is required to defeat these barbarians. We must leave by dawn."

"Lord Lancelot, I beseech you, stand and fight. The Highlanders stand with us. Together, we have already defeated almost ten thousand, even though they were slaves sent to war, broken by evil, torture and without a will to live. But it shows that we can fight, if only we decide. Now, I'm begging you, my lord, for all that is good in this world, for peace, we must fight."

Lancelot shook his head.

"There can no peace, no triumph against the Huns. Roman legions, Frankish spirit, and Demetian warriors have already fallen to them. Nothing can stop them now but a miracle. I'm sorry, Arthur, Merlin, but I will not risk the lives of my people for a glimmer that is too dim. Stay for the night, if you will. But by the morrow, my people will have left."

Arthur stood silent before the lord of Rodwin, regretful.

Closing his eyes, he held back the pain and loss he was enduring.

"That vision you saw," Merlin said, "has been seen by all the lords of Britannia. They will either join us, or all will fall."

Merlin turned, his robe glowing crimson as he strode

toward the doors. The guards opened them, and Arthur turned to follow.

By dawn, six days would remain till forty thousand Huns reached Demetia.

C.J. BROWN

16

PERIL FROM THE NORTH

WITH SUNRISE, THE HUN ARMIES assembled before the walls of Pittentrail.

The expendables amassed as a line of ten thousand, armed with weapons of all kinds, boasting shields of Gallic tribes and helmets of Germanic, Roman, and Gaulish origin.

Franks, Romans, Italians, Illyrians, Prussians, and Danes, enslaved, tortured, broken, stood before the ranks of true Huns, screaming, shrieking as dawn broke over the horizon. Beating their shields, they watched Gallagher as he thundered by the first rank, clad in Roman armor.

"Huns!" He shouted. "Warriors! The greatest the world has ever seen, today you fight for your king, for

101

your people, for the Empire! The finest race of godlike blood, you are the chosen ones!"

Roars echoed off the mountains, spilling out over the mountain pass as the barbarians cheered, and Fergus watched from the walls, disgusted.

"The lands of Demetia lay open! All the isle shall fall! Forty thousand men, led by an able general, march north, laying waste to the land. So, you must do the same, must do better! Raid every town! Slay every man. Steal every coin! Blood and glory await you!"

Again, they cheered, setting the Highlander destriers and other horses to rearing and neighing.

"I am Bishkar!" He shouted, to Fergus' surprise. "As a general of Attila's armies, I wear the armor of the accursed heir to the Roman Empire, gifted to me by the king of Caledonia! As a Roman and a Hun, I will lead you to victory!"

The Huns shrieked, drumming their shields. Hun banners streamed in the morning wind as the thunder of twenty thousand men shouted.

"Half of the true Huns will remain here!" Bishkar went on. "Protect Pittentrail from our enemies!"

At once, half of the true Huns raised their spears and swords, while the expendables stood quiet as Bishkar charged past them, toward the first rank of Huns.

Signalmen were there, and Bishkar nodded.

At once, they raised the flags and the drums of war beat as the expendables began marching forward.

Fergus watched, angry, as fifteen thousand men began marching toward the mountain pass. Three thousand cavalry charged toward the perilous road while the expendables began running and the Huns followed. Highlander horses pulled trebuchets alongside them, thundering ahead.

The black and gold banner of the Huns streamed amidst the barbarian force as they reached the mountain pass and began streaming from the field, leaving five thousand Huns in the trenches and the wooden outpost built outside the gates of Pittentrail.

Like roaches running from a boot, the Hun army thundered towards the pass, Bishkar charging amongst them.

As they raced across the mountain, Fergus turned from the battlements and looked out at his city.

The garrison, guarding the streets of the city from the treacherous Huns, all stared at him. Civilians, too, stared through their windows, angry and hateful.

C.J. BROWN

17

FIELDS OF BRITTANIA

TIBERIUS SURVEYED THE LAND AS his legionaries marched behind. Where green grass once was, there were only burned fields and dirt. Towns were burning, billowing columns of smoke. A Demetian banner was stuck in the ground, tattered, surrounded by fallen warriors.

Wagons lay overturned beside horses as the Roman legion traversed the field of fire and desolation.

Spears bristled beside arrows and swords littered the ground. Some of the soldiers were sick, throwing up as they witnessed the trail of destruction the Huns had left behind.

Tiberius felt himself hating the Huns and pitying the people of Britannia.

"No," he said to himself. "This is your path to the throne."

He shook off the thought as they passed a series of burning huts, others collapsed as piles of wood and ash.

In the distance, the ruins of a stone city could be seen burning, its walls crumbled.

As the Romans issued from the ridge, they saw the great city of Egolith, known even by the Romans of Italy. Its stone walls scorched by fire, the crumbled bricks piled amidst fallen cavalry and soldiers, heroes who defended their home from the greatest threat they had ever encountered.

Huns numbered less than the Demetians as the latter's banners lay burned and crumpled in the mud.

Rains were flooding the craters where stones hurled from catapults had struck the ground.

The five thousand Romans closed their eyes to the destruction as they marched north.

They saw nothing but the same for the next three days.

18

CALL TO ARMS

ARTHUR AND MERLIN SAT ASTRIDE by the main gate as they watched a long train of Rodwin soldiers and cavalry issue from the city, leading a column of civilians, wagons, and horses out. They were headed west, to the trading port, free to all.

"A rider and a hundred horse race to Demetia," Merlin announced.

Arthur turned to him, surprised.

Looking around, he tried to spot them, and saw them charging with all haste.

Arthur turned and broke into a gallop, leading Merlin and the fifty Demetian riders away from the city.

As they drew near to the strangers' column, Arthur heard Merlin's voice.

"He who leads them is Lord Galahad. He intends to speak with my father."

"Will he join us?"

"He is afraid. He will try to convince my father to bargain with Attila."

Arthur shouted and raced toward the lord of Astavon.

Within moments, as the Demetians thundered onto the road, some of the Astavonian men turned to see the Demetians chasing.

Shouts erupted and the column halted, dust kicked up by the horses swirling around them.

Arthur stopped, spotting Lord Galahad as Boadicea reared and Merlin stopped beside him, the rest of the Demetians stopping around them.

"Merlin!" Galahad shouted. "It was you who showed me that vision."

His voice was a baritone rumble, his face grim.

"Yes," Merlin said. "You wish to convince my father to make a deal with the Huns."

"There is no other way!"

"There is," Arthur objected, trotting toward him. "Stand and fight. Unite as one, all the tribes of Britannia."

Galahad looked at Arthur like he was looking upon a madman.

"There is no hope against the Huns. If these things have already happened, and if this is what they are capable of, there is nothing that can stop them. The Franks fell. King Fergus has joined them. The isle is crawling with these barbarians. The tribes are distant. Some haven't sent even messengers to each other in decades. There might be hope in unity, but there is no hope for that itself. The only way is to make peace."

"But the Huns will not accept that!" Arthur shouted. "They are a vile people. Peace goes against everything they believe. War is their source of life, repose and peace their bane."

"Then it would be wise to flee. You ought to as well, but first, we will try to strike a deal."

"Don't you understand?" Arthur screamed, one Roman general who had battled the Huns for years, seen their rise over the last two decades, to a lord who had not seen war at all. "They will only accept allegiance, and I don't think you or your people would be willing to align with them."

Galahad eyed him with anger.

Without a word, he turned and galloped off, headed for Demetia.

His train followed, leaving Arthur with his cloak swirling amidst the dust.

Shouting in anger, Arthur broke into a gallop and chased Galahad, followed by Merlin and the rest.

By mid-day, the horn of the city guard sounded as the Demetians and Astavonians thundered through the enchanted wood. They halted at the limits of the city, where King Megolin and Igraine were to receive Lord Galahad and their own kin.

Arthur and Merlin halted in the courtyard of the city guard, their horses striking the scorched cobblestone ground as the visitors strode in amidst broken buildings and piles of rubble.

Lord Galahad stopped before King Megolin and vaulted off.

He bowed, his cloak, bearing the rose crest of his house, flowing from his clasps.

Removing his helm as his men bowed, he rose.

"Your Grace," he said to Megolin.

"Lady…"

"Igraine," Arthur's mother said.

"Lady Igraine."

Turning back to Megolin, he said, "I have already met your son and this stranger."

"He is Arthur," Megolin at once responded, "son of Uther Pendragon, former heir to the Roman Empire, and my nephew."

Everyone gasped at that, and even Arthur grew unsteady, aware of it, though it wasn't real for him until now.

Within moments, King Megolin was listening in regret to the lord of Astavon, along with the members of his court, Igraine, Merlin, Magi Ro Hul, and Arthur.

"Concluding peace with them is the only way the

peoples of the isle can survive," Galahad argued, the goblet of wine in his hand.

"Do you see no other way?" Megolin asked. "No way we could put aside petty differences, old wounds, and band together against a real threat?"

Lord Galahad looked away.

"I'm sorry," he said.

"Fine then."

"Your Grace?" Arthur said.

"We cannot force these people, Arthur. That won't be unity, that will only be tyranny. Do as you will, Lord Galahad," he said, turning back to his fellow ruler. "Look after your people, but I advise you, fleeing is better than signing a peace with them."

Galahad bowed.

"Thank you, Your Grace. These are dark days. Perhaps, we may see the day when the peoples of the isle finally unite as one."

Megolin nodded.

Galahad bid farewell to the royals and the court, Arthur, then turned and left.

"The horizon is bleak," Magi Ro Hul said.

"There is hope left," Igraine said. "Even if the other tribes do not join us, we will stand against the enemy. If we fall, know that it isn't the end. We fight to defend this land because it is worth defending, not because it's all there is."

"Aunt Igraine is right," Merlin said. "Do not let fear cloud your spirit, friend."

Magi Ro Hul shook his head. "You may be wiser than most!" he shouted. "But you have not felt grief, nor pain, nor war. No vision will ever teach it to you. You know nothing of the world."

Magi Ro Hul turned and stormed out before anyone could say another word.

"He is a good man," Megolin said. "He is right to fear."

Arthur looked on at the scene, realizing he did not want to look at the fireplace, as now flames reminded him not of warmth and comfort, but of war and destruction.

"Forgive me, Mother, Your Grace, Merlin, but I must speak with my father."

They nodded.

"Arthur," Igraine said, "remember, you are his son. Your father is still there, somewhere. You need to help him get past his pain. No one but you can."

Arthur nodded, a tear rolling from his eye.

He turned and walked briskly to the doors. The guards opened them, and he left, headed to the palace adjacent to the great hall.

With hurried steps, he arrived before the doors of his father's chambers.

"Open the doors," Arthur told the guards, and at once they unlocked them and pushed them open.

Darkness, but for the candles placed outside his

window, suspended from an iron bar, and placed there by orders from Igraine.

Uther was sitting on his straw bed, staring out at the fires of the candles.

"Father," Arthur said, letting his tears flow.

Uther turned, his eyes burning with anger and pain.

"Gallagher is my son, the name she and I decided on before I left," he said, his voice quiet and heavy with pain.

"Father, you are trying to right your wrongs. But I too am your son. Can you not see that? Can you not see that I and Mother have stood by your side since the beginning? No one hates you. But you have to leave the pain behind, or else you will only live to bear more regrets."

"You are my flesh and blood," Uther said. "I want to let this go, but I cannot. What I did is worse than any could possibly do. For a throne, a chair that has caused the empire pain for so long, that has caused people and families chaos, I killed my family. I thought I did and did not plan to spare them. So, Gallagher may have lived, but as far as I'm concerned, I killed my own flesh and blood."

"Everyone makes mistakes, does things they regret for the rest of their lives, but that doesn't mean they're bad people. You know of the Hun general Alabar who defected from their ranks to join Rome without any weapons or men. From a sea of barbarians, there was one who saw truth. By that alone, he redeemed himself. And so, you are aware of your mistakes. That has redeemed you."

"No, Arthur," Uther said, tears rolling from his eyes. "I can never be redeemed. What I did it is beyond forgiving."

Arthur sniffled.

"I am your son also," Arthur said, "and Mother the woman you love. You are a man of honor, Father, of justice and wisdom. Gallagher is not. Grandfather was wrong to ask you to do what you did, but that's because he was a corrupt man. You are not so."

"You speak kindly to me, my son," Uther said, smiling sadly, "but there is nothing you can do. I must stand beside my son, beside the demon I created. I ask you to flee. You will have to run for the rest of your life, but I will not see the day when I am responsible for my own son's death. Please, do not give me more sorrow."

A rap of knuckles on the door shook Arthur and Uther out of their thoughts.

"Lord Arthur, a crow just arrived, sent from Astavon. The city has been attacked and overrun. The people are fleeing. They are requesting aid."

Arthur turned to Uther.

"Forgive me, Father," he said, then turned and left, followed by the royal guard as he hurried toward the steps.

Racing out into the open, the sound of horses neighing and hooves striking the cobblestone road echoed as a column of cavalry trotted to the limits of the city.

Horns and trumpets were ringing as commanders shouted orders and three thousand men, including the Romans who followed Arthur from the continent, filed through the streets, amassing in the courtyard and along the city limits.

Megolin was standing before the great doors of the great hall.

"Your Grace," Arthur shouted over the sound of an army preparing for war, "you plan to rescue the Astavonians. I stand with you."

"I knew you would," Igraine said.

Arthur nodded.

"Boadicea," Verovingian suddenly said.

He was no squire, or aid, but Verovingian had chosen to be by Arthur's side since the beginning. For that, Arthur was grateful.

"Thank you, my friend," Arthur said, and vaulted up onto his horse.

"Mother," he said, "Father is almost home."

Igraine nodded, tears welling in her eyes.

"You are a fine man, Arthur," Megolin said. "Were you king of a land, we would bow."

Arthur noticed Merlin smirking beside his father.

"Please, I do not want any adulation."

"You are wise, little man!" Magi Ro Hul bellowed.

Arthur turned and saw him approaching with his horse.

"A man who does not care for adulation is a true leader, a man of true honor. Fellows like King Megolin here don't bother to change tradition, so they just accept it, but they don't like it either."

He turned to Merlin.

"Please accept my apology. I was just afraid."

"No need. Your strange hair is a sight enough to chase away all woes."

Arthur chuckled, the first time he'd laughed in days.

More than anything else, the promise of his father, finally returning to him, had raised his spirits. But the horizon was still dark. By this point, counting the fallen, and including the fresh recruits from the continent, seventy thousand Huns had marched on Britannia. "Magi Ro Hul," Arthur said, turning serious, "you will lead the cavalry. Like Hannibal at the Battle of Cannae, I will lead the infantry against the Huns, then you target their cavalry, rout them, and then return and attack the infantry. But free the prisoners of Astavon first."

"Very good, my lord," Magi Ro Hul said and galloped off to the courtyard, where the cavalry was amassing.

Merlin jumped up onto his horse as a column of Demetian warriors marched through the street.

"I shall speak with your father while you are gone," Igraine said. "I am a reminder of his pain, but from you I feel I may now see him."

"Indeed," Arthur agreed. "He needs everyone who cares about him now. Bulanid is the last person he needs to see."

Igraine nodded.

"Farewell, Mother, Your Grace. Should I not return, please, do not let father fade."

"Rest assured, Arthur," Megolin said, his voice serious, "if it be my last act alive, I will see it done."

"I too will spare nothing to save our family," Igraine said, holding back the tears at the prospect of losing both her son and her husband.

Arthur was about to say something else, but he could not, and turned away.

Silent, he trotted off, followed by Merlin as they passed along the column.

"Arthur," he suddenly heard Olivie's voice say.

Arthur stopped, looking around in shock.

"Olivie?" he said, his voice breaking.

"Arthur, I am here. I have always been here."

Arthur found himself weeping uncontrollably as the Demetian warriors marched by.

"Do not cry, my love," Olivie said. "I am still with you. Merlin is channeling my spirit to you. He hopes I can give you strength before the most perilous battle of your life."

"You do," Arthur said, his weeping stopping.

"You are a good man, Arthur. You are grieving, you are in pain. Do not be. I will always be with you. Your Father will return. Good will triumph. Since I passed, I have spent the time seeing through history, and the thing I have found is that the universe will always tend to good. Evil will fall, as it always has. Though hope seems out of reach, and we face the end, our cause will triumph."

Arthur straightened and wiped away his tears.

"I miss you, Olivie."

"I miss you too, Arthur."

"What do I say to your father? He stands with the Huns."

"That might be so, but I know my father. He will not stray from good forever. He has seen things most should never have to know. His father was king during The Great War. At just eighteen, my father led an army of twenty thousand against the Demetians and Astavonians. It was worse than any battle he had ever fought. Fifty thousand fell that day. It was almost the end of the war. Grandfather and Grandmother told me told me that he was never the same after that. My mother was around to see the prince of Caledonia transform from a happy, naive boy to a disillusioned, quiet, and depressed man of war. He understands the terrors of war and will not see them repeat."

Arthur nodded.

"For him, trust in time."

"You know him better than I do," Arthur said.

"I do," Olivie chuckled.

"Thank you, my love."

Arthur turned and saw Merlin staring at him.

He nodded, and the warlock nodded back.

Then they rode toward the wood-line, by the city guard posts that had been built since Bulanid had attacked.

Five thousand Highlander, Roman, and Demetian

infantry stood before him, their spears pointed to the skies as pennons and banners streamed in the evening breeze.

The horns and trumpets ceased blaring as Magi Ro Hul sat before the cavalry of Demetia and Pittentrail.

Merlin waited before them, looking at Arthur.

His Demetian cloak flowing from his shoulders, he eyed the men before him.

"Soldiers!" He shouted, "Warriors of the isle! Today we march to save a people from the wave of darkness that washes over this green land. The city of Astavon has been overrun, its people driven off, its armies broken. For God, for good, for brothers, fathers, wives, and for the generations who shall rise after we are gone, we will save them, and we will defeat the Huns!"

"Yah!" The soldiers shouted, and the city resounded with cheers as every warrior and citizen within range of Arthur's voice roared.

Arthur drew his sword.

"Follow not me!" he bellowed. "Only your hearts and honor!"

Again, they cheered, raising their spears to the sky.

Arthur eyed the honorable men who stood before him.

Merlin was smiling, his cloak glowing purple.

Arthur, his soul renewed, turned his horse around and trotted forward, followed by five thousand men who marched after him. Thundering through the enchanted wood as Magi Ro Hul lead the cavalry out of the city, they emerged from the trees.

C.J. BROWN

19

SPIRIT OF ROME

TIBERIUS AND HIS MEN HAD utterly changed since they landed on the shores of Britannia.

"The stories of the Germanic tribes across the continent paled in comparison to the destruction the Huns had brought to the plains of Britannia.

His men reviled the Huns, as much as he did, but Tiberius wanted the throne. He had since he was first appointed commander of a century within leagues of the Rhine and battled the Huns, winning every time. Rising to the rank of general within five years, he had led several campaigns against the barbarians, and his name was known by every Hun. For them to now be aligned with a common goal was disgusting to both them and himself.

But for Tiberius, anything was worth it for the throne of Rome.

Three days after they passed the ruins of Egolith, Tiberius now spotted the Hun camp, a tent city with fires burning before them, as far as the eye could see.

We will set up camp here, Tiberius ordered.

Within an hour, the legionnaires had set up their own tents and the Roman banner streamed in the wind, the air polluted with smoke and ash. A town burned within sight of the Hun camp, while the barbarians drank and ate, marveling at the gold and coin they'd looted.

"We will not meet with them," Tiberius declared. "We will not deal with them. We march only with them."

"Aye, my lord," one of the centurions said, his eagle staff pointed to the sky. "They are vile."

"Do not fret, my friend," Tiberius said, "for we will defeat them once our goals are achieved."

Sunset saw the Roman army watch the Huns with anger and hatred.

By dawn, the two armies, enemies since the beginning of time, marched north.

Tiberius did not deign to look at the Huns as they shouted insults at his legion. He knew none of his men were as undisciplined as the Huns to fly to arms at an insult, and so did not bother ordering them to keep their formation. The Romans did not care to be insulted by Huns and marched on without reply.

By mid-day, the Huns and Romans reached a town

where the garrison stood ready for battle, Demetian banners streaming in the wind.

Without a word, without even thought, Tiberius thundered away from his legion, racing ahead of the Hun army.

"Soldiers of Demetia!" He bellowed. "I beseech you! Surrender your arms and the city, and your people will be kept safe. I have seen the destruction these Huns leave behind. I wish not the same fate for you!"

The Huns heard the Roman general with anger as he tried to make their capture of the city peaceful.

"Hah!" The cavalry captain shouted. "A Roman general marching with Huns! What could be any more reviling?"

The Demetian warriors shouted agreement, and Tiberius felt his anger rising.

"Please, do not fight. You have not seen what the Huns are capable of."

The captain eyed him angrily.

"We will not trust any who stand with these barbarians, the dregs of the world."

Tiberius looked at him with sorrow.

"Then I am sorry," he said and galloped away.

"We will take no part in this!" He shouted to his men as he returned to his legion. "We will take no part in this."

C.J. BROWN

20

TREACHERY

A MESSENGER RAN TOWARD THE PALACE, weary with travel. The soles of his sandals striking the cobblestone path as he reached the palace of the Franks, he ran up the steps to the doors and burst through. He ran for Attila's throne room.

"Running through the open doors, he dropped to his knee, thirty yards from his king.

"Sire," he said, "Gerlach calls you to join him in Britannia. His armies have laid waste to the land, turning it befitting of a Hun king. They are four days from Demetia, the capital city of the first kingdom of Britannia. Bishkar has sent word. He acknowledges Gerlach as general and leads the men who landed at Dornoch from Le Havre

125

against the tribes of Britannia. Gerlach also forwarded Bishkar's message. He says he found out Lispania was planning to betray you, so he allied with the local Caledonians and slew him."

"Perhaps that was good. Lispania was always snake," Attila sighed.

"I will prepare to leave at once and will depart for Britannia by sunset. Rogarth," he said, turning to one of his main advisors, "you will govern the empire and lead our forces here while I am away. Begin preparations for the war with Rome. If things are proceeding as planned, we will be ready to strike soon. Send twenty thousand men to Ostia. Eventually, a greater army will augment them. Have them ready to march on Rome."

Rogarth bowed as the messenger left by the great doors.

21

THE FACE OF HONOR

ARTHUR LED FIVE THOUSAND MEN north as Magi Ro Hul charged ahead with Highlander and Demetian cavalry.

"The Demetian and Highlander soldiers running behind Arthur kept pace as they thundered toward the city of Astavon that guarded the North River. Green fields and cities not yet attacked by the Huns flew by as they charged north.

Arthur found himself returning to his own. Anger and hate no longer powered his movements, only honor and the principles of loyalty, family, and peace.

The men behind him were greater than any legionary

Arthur had ever known, except for the ones he had led for his last years fighting for Rome.

Now, with the Demetians and Highlanders, the thousand Romans who had made it to Inver Ridge marched to war against the Huns who threatened the freedom of the isle and the continent.

Sunset saw the Demetian, Highlander, and Roman army walk as they ate, then break into a run again, fueled by urgency and a call to duty.

By midnight, the fires that burned around Astavon could be seen from a league away.

Smoke spiraled up and drifted toward them as they advanced along the river, now walking towards the city.

The roar of the barbarians could be heard as Magi Ro Hul split his cavalry into two and they began charging far off. Arthur watched them halt, an army of blue, yellow, and red waiting as they eyed the muddy plains, shielding their noses from smoke and fumes that rose from the ground. The city of Astavon was crawling with Huns. Lord Galahad and his people were caged with wood and iron, while groups of a hundred at a time were trained as expendables.

Others were fashioning swords and axes by roaring furnaces, slashed with ropes.

Arthur felt his rage rising, but quickly displaced his emotion with thought.

He raised his hand, signaling for the men to amass as planned.

At once, the soldiers began forming a close mass and the front line was a row of a thousand shields.

Archers stood behind the shield wall, ready to send a sheet of arrows racing up into the night sky.

Behind them, rank upon rank of Romans, Demetians, and Highlanders stood ready to fight the Huns.

"Arthur strode forward. The Huns would be able to see them if only they looked.

He drew his sword, its blade glistening in the light of flames, stars, and the moon.

Pointed toward the heavens, he swung it down.

At once, the archers loosed their arrows and five hundred flew up.

Whistling through the air, they almost dimmed the light of the moon when commotion erupted across the Hun camp and the arrows fell on the enemy.

Arthur stood where he was as the Hun army quickly prepared to fight back.

"Archers!" A captain shouted.

Another shower of arrows rose up from the ground and streaked across the sky as Magi Ro Hul began leading the western cavalry toward the Hun riders struggling to organize. At once, the other cavalry set off, thundering toward the Huns.

Shouts sounded as the enemy formed up, facing the Britannian forces.

Another round of arrows raced up and fell on the

Huns, cutting down a thousand as the rest charged toward the shield wall.

"Hold the line!" Arthur bellowed, keeping steady.

Merlin was beside him, his greatsword that did not slay drawn.

The thunder of five thousand true Huns racing toward them grew louder as the barbarians shrieked and howled.

Near the ruins of Astavon, catapults hurled balls of flame and stone toward Arthur's men as Magi Ro Hul clashed with the Hun cavalry and cornered the expendables to keep them from attacking. Arthur had no plans to kill them. The only sin he had committed fighting the Huns had been not freeing the expendables from their oppressors.

The line of Huns crashed into the shield wall, falling one by one as the Highlander infantry swung their blades.

Arthur slashed around him as Merlin incapacitated men attempting to break the line.

Where fireballs were streaking toward them, the infantry cleared only that piece of land to avoid the projectiles.

Arthur, remaining where he had stopped a few minutes past, found the plains swarming with the enemy, more ruthless than they had ever been, viler than the slaves they sent to weaken the ranks of their opponents.

Shouts were sounding from his men as they struggled to maintain the shield wall.

Archers picked off Huns from behind, but the line was slowly breaking. Soldiers fell with their shields.

Fires set the grass amidst the formation to burning, and the soldiers not yet fighting tried to douse the flames with their cloaks.

Snow was not yet falling, but the cold was relentless, and soldiers without their cloaks found themselves pale.

Arthur's arm burned as he cut down Huns all around him as they tried to slay him and his horse.

Merlin was fighting with all the strength of a Demetian prince and warlock, focused on the task before him.

Bodies piled before the line of Highlanders as the Huns continued to attack them.

Arthur was shaken out of his duel with a hulking Hun shrieking like a madman by shouts erupting from the western flank.

Hun infantry were plowing through the ranks, advancing with almost no difficulty.

Demetian, Roman, and Highlander banners fell to the ground as the Hun army broke the formation in two.

"Stay close!" Arthur bellowed as he cut down the shrieking Hun.

Near the city, the fighting between the Hun cavalry and Magi Ro Hul's forces was raging. The citizens of Astavon and Lord Galahad had been freed from their prison and armed themselves with the Huns' weapons. Fighting beside the cavalry, they cut down the Huns.

But the infantry was failing, and Arthur could do nothing, overwhelmed himself by hundreds of Huns attacking the shield wall.

Almost a thousand of his men had fallen before Arthur turned to see Magi Ro Hul leading his cavalry to defeat the enemy.

Magi Ro Hul slashed at the first Hun soldier as his men collided with the ranks of Huns plowing through Arthur's men.

They cheered, and Arthur shouted in relief as he cut down another Hun.

Within an hour, four thousand Huns lay dead, but only a thousand of Arthur's men still lived. Magi Ro Hul's cavalry had been reduced to two thousand, and the remaining thousand Huns were retreating, abandoning Astavon.

Arthur watched the barbarians flee.

Tired, battle-weary, his arm afire, Arthur dropped from his horse.

Merlin stood beside him, physically unfazed.

Magi Ro Hul was in the distance, looking at the people of Astavon, the children, the old, the sick, all wielding swords. He hated that people as old as grandfathers and as pure as children, had had to see the terrors of war.

"Are you all right?" Merlin asked Arthur.

"Yes," Arthur nodded.

Rising back up, he walked to where he saw Lord Galahad standing amongst his people and the remaining soldiers of his army who had tried to break the first Hun attack that morning.

His helmet by his side, Arthur walked past the

fallen banners and the soldiers roaming the field. The expendables had surrendered and were being led away, not shackled or tortured. He could hear their voices as the Highlanders, Romans, and Demetians shared their food and drink with them.

"Lord Galahad," Arthur said, walking up to him, his tunic stained with dirt and blood, his hair tousled and his eyes alert.

He turned to see Arthur.

Surprise seized him.

"You rescued us," he said, "even though I would not join you."

"I am not a tyrant," Arthur responded. "I may be heir to the throne of Rome, but I am not like any emperor of the past. In fact, I wish not even to be. Your people are good. You are just. I understand why you would want to strike a deal or flee."

"Perhaps I am of a different mind now," he said.

Arthur looked at him.

"What do you mean?"

"You have shown me that there is hope against the Huns. Triumph is achieved with great cost, but none of these people died in vain. Because of them, our enemy is weakened. I thereby pledge allegiance to you. Astavon will see the day when Britannia is united and rid of these barbarians. If you shall plan that we one day march to liberate the continent from the Huns, we shall march with you."

Arthur did not know how to respond, except to nod.

"Thank you, Lord Galahad. Britannia owes much to you for your unity alone."

Galahad bowed.

"Those expendables," Arthur said, looking to they who were once slaves of the Huns, "they are not true Huns. They are Franks, Romans, Britannians, Illyrians, free peoples. They are not our enemy, but our allies. We have freed them, and should they choose, they will march with us against the Huns."

Galahad nodded. "Very good," he said.

Magi Ro Hul arrived by their side. "Arthur, he said, the men are ready to return, and the freedmen will follow."

"Lord Galahad," he turned to the guardian of Astavon, "your people fought bravely today. Fifty years ago, my people and yours once fought against each other. I hope that is left behind us, and we can unite at the dawn of a new age."

"Aye," Galahad said.

Magi Ro Hul nodded.

Arthur was about to say something when he fell to the ground, his eyes white and glowing.

"I was wrong," Merlin said, his voice grim for the first time. "The Huns have reached Demetia."

Arthur's eyes darted back and forth as he saw Hun armies setting the enchanted wood ablaze. Trebuchets hurled fire and stone at the city as King Megolin and General Clyde fought to hold back the barbarians.

Arthur's eyes closed and he sat there, his face distant and disturbed.

"The Huns are attacking Demetia," he said, and Magi Ro Hul's face turned pale.

"Charge!" Arthur shouted, turning and running for his horse.

Magi Ro Hul's voice boomed across the plains as Galahad led his people, now armored and armed, to the horses left behind by the Huns.

The freedmen, though still dressed as they had been, had torn off the Hun insignia and began charging after the cavalry as Magi Ro Hul led them back the way they arrived.

Arthur vaulted up onto his horse and charged, not even worrying about the army as twenty-three thousand souls thundered after him, leaving the burning plains of Astavon behind, guarded by a thousand Astavonians who swore to never let the Huns pass there again.

Charging faster than they ever had, the armies of a united people spotted the fires that burned around Demetia two hours before dawn.

The Hun army was surrounding the city. Fifty thousand barbarians charged the ranks of the Demetian defenders as catapults sent fire and stone hurling through the air. Showers of arrows rose up from the wood and the city as tar and fire lit up the ranks of Huns who fought to fell every last Demetian warrior.

Arthur, enraged, led his twenty-three thousand men across the plain.

Archers began loosing arrows at the enemy as an army of shrieking Huns broke off to fight the Britannians.

The two armies collided less than a hundred yards from the wood.

Arthur slashed with his sword, breaking armor and shields as the fury of people and soldiers battled the barbarians.

Magi Ro Hul fought beside him as Merlin struck with his blade. Fireballs streaked across the predawn sky as the sun approached the horizon.

Dawn broke to see the fire of the enchanted forest unstoppable and uncontrollable. Galahad was leading a cavalry while Magi Ro Hul attacked the Huns' western flank and Arthur redoubled the attack against the center force.

As Arthur cut down one of them, sunlight shining off his iron armor, he looked up and spotted a hulking giant watching the battle.

Three hundred yards away, the enemy commander was the very embodiment of the vile Huns. Arthur, his horse rearing, realized he had to fight him later.

With five thousand men behind him, they were able to clear a path to the city.

With the sun rising over the horizon, night was receding, but the darkness had not left. Fires raged as soldiers lay in the dirt, banners left abandoned on the ground and arrows and spears bristling.

Reaching the burning forest, Arthur spotted a cavalry column charging out of the wood, slashing at the enemy as their horses reared and fireballs streaked overhead.

Something about the commander felt familiar, as he fought the enemy, his helmet missing.

"Father," Arthur said, tears welling in his eyes, hope rekindled in his heart.

"Yah!" He shouted and Merlin turned to see Uther Pendragon battling the enemy.

"Your father has returned," Merlin said, the sound of battle surrounding them.

"We fight as one," Arthur declared.

Turning, he charged to his father's side, with Merlin just behind.

Soldiers on foot clashed with the barbarians amidst the forest while Arthur led a thousand men to his father's side.

"Son!" Uther shouted, when he turned and saw his son approaching him.

Arthur stopped before Uther's destrier.

He nodded, and Uther turned back to the enemy.

"Long have these Huns caused the world pain and agony. No more."

Arthur almost laughed as they galloped off and clashed with the enemy again.

The forces of Demetia collided with the Hun ranks,

sparing nothing. All efforts were directed toward defeating the barbarians. No matter what, they had sworn they would not let them pass.

Catapults hurled burning grass and boulders through the air.

Arthur and Uther fought side by side as King Megolin and General Clyde fought to free the trees from the enemy.

Arthur slashed, arrows racing past, as his horse reared. Beside him, his father was cutting down Huns with all the fury of a Roman general, and an emperor. Like Augustus and Caesar who fought with their men, the courage Uther inspired in all was unparalleled.

Within minutes, the Hun infantry phalanx directly ahead of the Hun commander watching from the distance was decimated, and Arthur looked up at him.

"Arthur! To the trees!" Uther shouted.

Arthur turned and followed, surrounded by friendly forces on foot and horse charging for the wood-line.

Spears were launched from the Britannian army as the sound of battle echoing through the burning forest was heard.

The smell of ash and smoke turned Arthur's nose and lungs sore as he charged toward the trees.

Dawn illuminated the muddy plain where green grass once flourished, where bunnies once ran. Thundering past the trees, Arthur slashed at a Hun. Jumping over a fallen tree, as more creaked, falling to the ground, branches breaking and men running, Arthur stayed by Uther with their four thousand men. Everywhere, Huns were dueling with their forces. No longer were formations clashing with armies. Soldiers were fighting for their lives.

Arthur could see Demetia through the flames and arrows. The courtyard was ablaze, a number of the guard towers collapsed. royal guards and Demetian warriors were battling the Huns, struggling to keep the enemy at bay till the rest of their forces could retake the streets and sectors that had already been lost.

His greatsword gleaming, his armor dented, Arthur found himself surrounded by Huns. With fear now powering his arms, he slashed at them, with no friends in sight.

Arrows and spears raced past as he tried to charge back to the city.

Clearing a path with his sword, he made his way to the courtyard.

A stone crashed into one of the barracks just then, sending brick and mortar flying out.

"Hold the line!" He heard a voice shout and turned to see King Megolin with a column of infantry and cavalry, guarding one of the streets that led to the rest of the city. The others being guarded by battalions of royal guards, civilians, and all their allies.

"Father," Arthur whispered.

He turned and galloped to King Megolin's side, spotting Uther amongst the first rank.

"The garrison has but three hundred men left," Megolin

shouted. "The reinforcements you brought are not able to reach us. They are being cornered beyond the wood. The Huns have already overrun most of the northern sector. The courtyard is all we hold here."

Arthur turned back as a commander shouted, "Loose!" and archers launched a shower of burning arrows at the enemy.

Tar was being hurled from the towers that remained as flaming arrows set a line of fire to burning, blocking the Huns from King Megolin.

"There is still hope," Arthur said. "Magi Ro Hul leads the army outside. We have to weaken the Huns where they control the wood. The royal guard can take care of the Huns here. We have to free up Magi Ro Hul!"

Megolin nodded.

"Royal guard!" He boomed, "defend the city!"

"At once, the royal guards amidst their ranks broke off, amassing as five hundred men, to attack the northern sector.

"Archers! Front line! Make way!"

Arthur, Megolin, Uther, and the rest of the men at the head of the column stepped aside to let the archers move through.

They loosed arrow after arrow at the Huns beyond the wall of fire.

Arthur sat steady by his uncle and father.

"Where's Mother?"

"She leads the royal guards already defending the northern sector. Two hundred warriors."

Arthur nodded.

"Father," he turned, "thank you."

"My son, I ask not for your forgiveness," he said, smiling sadly, black marks streaked across his face. "Thank you for being my son."

Arthur nodded, unable to reply and turned back to the line of fire.

Archers were loosing arrows at the enemy, when the first Hun ran through the fire.

One by one, they darted through the flames, not caring for the heat or the pain.

Arthur raised his sword and cut down the first one as hundreds poured in.

Thundering over the cobblestone, they stormed the towers and the buildings as Arthur, Uther, Megolin, and Clyde fought to hold the line.

As Arthur slashed at a Hun, his eyes blue, his face pale and dirty, an arrow broke through his iron armor and flesh.

Burrowing into his lung, he felt blood rush in as he struggled to breathe.

Uther suddenly eyed his son.

"Arthur!" he shouted.

Arthur turned to him, trying to breathe.

"I'm fine," he said, cutting down another Hun.

Another arrow hit him in the shoulder.

Uther at once jumped in front of his son, dressed in his Roman armor.

Arthur felt his vision growing blurry but remembered Olivie's voice, remembered that his father was fighting beside him, fighting to save him, that good and honest men stood with him, that the cause he was now bleeding for was the greatest he'd ever fought for.

Shaking himself out of his blurriness, he turned and cut down a Hun.

His right shoulder burned from the arrow wound, but he ignored the pain and kept fighting.

He looked up and saw a stone racing toward them.

"Move aside!" He shouted.

Darting away, soldiers cleared behind him to avoid the rock.

It landed, breaking off a few pieces and sending them flying through the air. Soldiers blocked with their shields as Hun arrows and spears raced toward them.

Men were shouting and some were beginning to flee.

"Stay together!" General Clyde bellowed.

Arthur, short of breath, kept slaying the Huns, one after another. Yet they kept attacking, running through the wall of fire that was now diminishing.

"Fall back!" Megolin shouted. "Make for the temple!"

At once, soldiers began running away from the courtyard as Clyde and Megolin followed.

Uther and Arthur turned, galloping away as the Huns overran the courtyard.

There was no place battle could not be seen, no street, no corner where there wasn't fighting.

Iron struck iron along the streets as the Huns redoubled their attack.

Fire and stone still streaked overhead, demolishing the buildings of Demetia.

Within moments, their hooves and soles striking the cobblestone road, the army reached the temple, where the citizens of Demetia prayed daily to Gaea.

"We defend this sacred land!" Megolin bellowed. "At all costs!"

Soldiers, many bleeding, their shields bristling with arrows, watched as the Huns thundered toward them, shrieking.

Archers loosed arrow after arrow, cutting down the ranks of the enemy as a few reached them.

Arthur slashed at one as the rest charged through the lines of their own dead.

Arthur's sword met a Hun shield, breaking through wicker and striking the barbarian.

As he fell, Arthur turned and cut down another Hun. Beside him, Uther, his strikes growing weaker, still fought.

A tower fell in the distance, the crash of stone and brick landing on the cobblestone road echoing through the streets. Shouts were sounding from across the city when commotion erupted behind him.

Arthur turned and saw a Hun column attacking his own, breaking the line.

Archers tried to pick off enemy warriors as they attacked the column, cutting down men with almost no difficulty, but it would not work.

Arthur turned and galloped across, cutting down one of the Huns who was breaking the column.

From the street that they attacked, Huns were storming the buildings.

The column Arthur now fought to defend was comprised of civilians, Romans, Demetians, and Highlanders. Standard-bearers used their banners to charge the enemy while swordsman swung their blades and axes. Archers cut down the enemy, but strength was finite, and the arrows were running out.

Within minutes, the column was broken. Each man was fighting for himself. Orders fell on deaf ears as Arthur felt his arm weakening.

Another arrow struck him, tearing through his shoulder from the back.

Pain sent him falling of his horse.

Clattering to the ground, soldiers running past him, Huns overrunning the street, Arthur felt his sight and hearing diminish.

"Arthur!" A voice bellowed.

He turned and saw Uther kneeling beside him. Then an arrow pierced Uther's chest.

"No!" Arthur screamed, his clarity of sight returned.

Uther looked at his son, tears welling in his eyes, and fell over.

"Father!" Arthur shouted, sitting by Uther.

Uther looked at him, his sword by his side.

"Forgive me, Arthur," he said, as a Hun ran past them. "You are my son. I only have one."

Arthur found himself weeping.

"You have made me proud. Your mother helped me see. Kindness, my son," he said, clinging to life, "heals all souls. I'm sorry I saw too late."

"No, Father," Arthur said crying, his wounds weakening him by the second. "This isn't the end. You still have time, laughs to share, tales to tell, family. This is not the end."

Uther chuckled, weakly.

"I'm sorry, my son," he said, holding his arm. "You have always been a Pendragon, the greatest of us. You shall always be."

His eyes grew distant.

"Father, no!" Arthur cried.

"Father!"

Arthur wept, kneeling beside his father.

The sound of battle disappeared as he sat there, all the pain he had ever felt rushing to his mind at the same time.

He remembered the pain his family had endured, the pain Bulanid Mehmet had caused, the pain Lucius caused, the pain Grandfather caused. But he also remembered the happiness, the closeness of his family. Never before had there been a more wholesome one. Uther had taught Arthur how to wield a sword, a spear, a bow, how to gallop, taught him the history of Rome and the deeds of great emperors, that he would one day be the emperor, and that he would be greater than even Augustus.

He felt hatred rising but remembered his father's words.

Conflict erupted between his hate and the words of his father.

Arthur was suddenly picked up and raised onto a horse.

"Father!" Arthur shouted.

"The city is lost," Merlin said. "We must retreat."

Arthur looked around and saw King Megolin charging ahead, with members of the royal guard and surviving warriors. Igraine was already there, leading a hundred elites.

Slumped over the neck of the great destrier, Arthur felt the pain of his wounds fading.

The sound of shrieking Huns, battle, and fire faded away.

Grief, sorrow, fear, anger, all occupied his mind.

He pictured Olivie, his father, his mother, Merlin, Megolin, Magi Ro Hul.

They were all there, smiling at him, laughing, happy. Jokes were being told, tales recounted. A future, a life that Arthur knew would never be. His mind drifted again, and he saw him marrying Olivie. Magi Ro Hul, his mother, father, uncle, cousin, they were all there. Vipsanius was standing by his side. A joyous laugh sounded, and Arthur smiled.

He almost wanted to say something, reach out, when all things faded away.

ALSO BY C.J. BROWN

PENDRAGON AND MERLIN'S TOMB

PENDRAGON AND THE MISTS OF

BRITTANIA

PENDRAGON AND THE TRAITOR'S

MENACE

NEWSLETTER

This is the fourth book in the Pendragon Legend. If you enjoyed Books 1-4, sign up for C.J. Brown's newsletter to get the first notice of new releases. You can sign up for the newsletter on C.J. Brown's website.

CJ-BROWN.COM

ABOUT THE AUTHOR

C.J. Brown has a lifelong passion for fantasy books, and she quit her career in marketing to pursue her dream of becoming an author. Legends and myths in particular strike her fancy, and she loves putting her own spin on them. An adventurer at heart, when not writing, she can be found exploring the old mystical Northwoods around her home, where she finds much of her inspiration.

Website: **cj-brown.com**
Facebook: **fb.me/cjbrown78**

Thanks for reading. Please consider leaving a review—it means a lot!

Printed in Great Britain
by Amazon

64215640R00095